FISHING FOR STONES

Glen R Stansfield

ISBN-13:978-0-9933118-0-2

To Jess

This is a work of fiction. Many of the places, people, situations and businesses in this book are real, but as far as the author is aware, none of the dialogue or actions in the story occurred. All other characters are fictitious and any resemblance to real persons either living or dead is purely co-incidental.

Acknowledgements

These are the people that in one way or another made this book possible. I wanted to 'get it right' as much as I could in a work of fiction. Only when the 'truth' is accurate can the 'lies' be made believable.

My thanks go to the following, and I hope I have not forgotten anyone;

Former Grampian Police Officers;

Geoff Marston, Douglas Donaldson, Norman MacClean, Neil Murray, Harry Thorburn, Antony Fraser.

John Mayhew, (NATS Aberdeen.)

Martin Bunce, (Bond Air Services.)

Davy Gow, (former work colleague at Bond Helicopters.)

Rob Jeffries, (Hon. Curator, Thames Police Museum, Wapping.)

Sue Noyes for her unceasing proofreading and editing.

Seumas Gallacher for his encouragement and invaluable advice.

And not least my wife Jess, who has had to listen to my prattlings for quite some time.

CHAPTER ONE

22nd February 1990, Near Longa, Angola

On the other side of the valley, five trucks were descending the steep slope to the bridge over the Cuiriri River: Russian built KrAZ. The convoy was still far enough away for them to get into an ambush position, and small enough for them to tackle.

The Major slowly lowered his binoculars, ensuring the sunlight could not reflect off the lenses and give him away to the enemy. Reconnaissance being their primary role, the standing orders still allowed for the attack of targets of opportunity, as long as it did not compromise their main duty of intelligence gathering. Under the cover of the tall grass he crawled up from the shallow foxhole, to where the rest of his group waited.

Parked on the opposite side of the ridge line, under a cluster of trees, the patrol's two 110 Land Rovers sat covered by camo netting to keep them hidden from occasional patrolling aircraft. They had chosen this place to lay up for a couple of days on the return journey to their operational base in Mavinga. With a clear view of the major highway between Menongue and Cuito Cuanavale, they observed the supply convoys passing between the two. Details of the movements would allow the intelligence unit to estimate the strength of the enemy in Cuito Cuanavale. This convoy was the first they had seen the Major thought small enough to be attacked by the eight-man patrol. He quickly briefed his men on its strength.

"Lead vehicle is carrying troops, fifteen at the most. The remaining vehicles are loaded with supplies. There may be someone riding shotgun in each truck but I can't tell at this range. We'll take them after the second bend this side of the river, a hundred metres west of where the trail joins the road. RPG to front and rear vehicles then mop up as necessary. Any questions?"

Several shakes of the head. They knew the drill. This would not be their first ambush. All were well trained, and they trusted the Major implicitly. He treated them well. Not like some of the other officers.

The heavily laden supply trucks used engine braking to slow them on the long descent to the river. The terrain in this part of Angola is characterised by a series of steep sided valleys cutting into a high plateau. Almost all the valleys run roughly north-south, carrying the rivers towards the Namibian border. The plateau is covered in a mixture of scrub, trees and grassland, some of the grass tall enough to hide a Land Rover, or even an armoured car.

On the other side of the river an equally steep climb awaited the convoy. The trucks would labour for several minutes until they reached the top of the valley, giving the group enough time to get into position for the ambush. Splitting into two teams of four they would position themselves far enough apart to be at opposite ends of the convoy as it passed. This would make it difficult for any survivors; the attack coming from two places, an effective tactic.

They left their camp and set off across the scrub towards a track leading to the main road; the grass kept down the dust. Once on the narrow track the convoy could not see them, which was just as well given the amount of dust they were now producing in their dash.

Although preparations seemed rushed, they had carefully chosen the ambush position. It was close to the camp with good cover on the north side of the road where they were, but little to the south. Situated between two bends, it was out of sight of any other vehicles there might be in the distance. They left the Land Rovers parked near to the highway under a tamarind tree, and close to the track. Ten minutes before the lead truck came into view around the curve; the two groups were in their respective ambush positions.

The Major breathed a sigh of relief; the vehicles still maintained their proximity to each other; exactly as he had observed them earlier on their descent. Far too close together in his opinion, making his task easier. The road dipped slightly here, and it provided an ideal location for the ambush. By hitting the convoy in this depression they had the advantage of elevation over the opposing force.

The RPG's fired simultaneously. A ball of fire erupted from the last truck as the round found its mark. At the front of the convoy things did not go as well. The Major watched in disbelief as the round from his own group's RPG passed through the open window of the truck. Under normal circumstances the downward trajectory from the team's firing position should have caused the grenade to hit the door on the other side of the truck, but by one of those strange twists of fate, one of the stabilising fins clipped the top of the window frame lifting the projectile enough for it to pass through the open window on the opposite side. Finally the grenade exploded on a tree some thirty metres beyond the truck.

The KrAZ remained unscathed; the same could not be said of the driver. A second stabilising fin had sliced through the driver's neck severing the carotid artery and trachea in its passage; he was now drowning in his own blood. In his panic he stamped hard on the brake pedal. The back wheels of the truck locked up on the loose gravel and the truck slewed sideways across the road. Taken by surprise the following driver swerved to the right but could not avoid hitting the rapidly decelerating truck on the rear corner. The impact had sufficient force to tip it on its side. The complement of troops clung desperately to sides of the stricken vehicle but several fell onto the road. It finally came to rest, but not before one unfortunate soldier was crushed, trapped under the truck as it slid to a halt.

For a moment nothing happened. The world seemed to pause to take stock of the situation.

The thudding sound and high pitch whine of AK-47 rounds hitting the ground next to his head brought the Major back into the real world.

"Merda! Cubanos."

The Major ducked down as the rounds found their mark where his head had been a moment ago. A shower of earth landed on his helmet.

These were not the expected MPLA soldiers but some of the Cuban troops remaining in Angola. What on earth were they doing here? The Cubans should not be this far south as part of the withdrawal agreement.

Shots were coming from the lead truck, and the Major became aware of the sound of his own team's Heckler & Koch G3 weapons; the second team providing them with covering fire having quickly dealt with the surviving truck drivers.

The last thing he wanted was to get into a fire-fight, but things do not always go to plan.

"Raol, get that bloody thing reloaded and hit that truck."

A quick glance told him he needn't have bothered. Raol had already reloaded and was lining up the weapon on the lead vehicle again. This time the grenade hit the front of it with devastating effect. The troops taking cover behind were either killed or badly wounded.

The AK-47 fire diminished but did not stop entirely. A few of the Cubans had taken refuge in the ditch at the roadside, instead of by the now fiercely burning KrAZ, although being on lower ground had put them at a disadvantage. They had to break cover to see up the slope towards the attackers, but this did not stop them from firing back at the ambushers.

The Major thought there were maybe four or five survivors in the ditch, but the smoke from the burning trucks billowing into the sky was causing him more concern. It was time to withdraw before someone noticed the thick black plumes. Longa airfield had Mi-8 helicopters and in Menongue, further to the West, a MiG fighter squadron was stationed. He did not intend to be around when they arrived to investigate.

He signalled to the second group to withdraw to the Land Rovers. As he turned to his own team he saw Raol slumped on the ground bleeding from his right shoulder; conscious but clearly in shock. He gave instructions to the other two soldiers to get the wounded man back to the Land Rover. He provided covering fire as the men dragged Raol to the vehicles. Once they were clear the Major followed, firing short bursts towards the surviving troops on the road to dissuade them from attempting anything heroic.

Back at the Land Rovers, he learned one member of the second team had also been wounded. He had taken a round in the leg. Neither of the wounds were bad, but they needed attention soon. Luckily, in both cases, the bullet had passed through without hitting any major arteries or bone. He was not happy about it though. None of his men had ever been wounded before and he felt fully responsible and saddened.

Failing to destroy the lead truck had almost turned the attack into a disaster. Had it not been for the collision between the two trucks the Cubans might have reacted quicker and overwhelmed the small reconnaissance group. Only Raol's quick reloading of the RPG had saved them from a difficult and protracted battle.

The Major surmised any searchers would be more likely to concentrate on the area to the south of the road, in the direction of the rebel stronghold. He elected to head west for several kilometres, on the north side and parallel to the highway, before turning south and home. It was a risky strategy; to the West was Longa and undoubtedly more Cuban troops, but he was certain the last thing they would expect was for his patrol to head towards them.

Thirty minutes later they crossed the main road without incident and headed south into the bush towards Mavinga.

He'd suffered enough of this. Whatever it took, the Major wanted to get out of this war, on his own two feet, and in one piece.

CHAPTER TWO

2nd March 1990, Boddam, Aberdeenshire

Three miles south of Peterhead lies the village of Boddam. Once a thriving fishing community, the village is now known more for the military installation of RAF Buchan, and the nearby Peterhead Power Station. In the harbour, the herring drifters and trawlers have given way to creel, ripper and leisure boats.

On the southern side of the village near to the military camp, and some sixty feet above the North Sea sits the former Earl's Lodge. In recent times it was a hotel until a fire destroyed the roof. Now it lies abandoned and in ruins. The building looks out on the rugged shoreline dominating the coast to the south of the village. Further to the South the cliffs sheer up from the shore, providing a breeding ground for seabirds. Below the hotel the cliffs are more accessible, and it is possible to clamber down the rocks to get nearer to the water; not the easiest thing to do when laden with fishing tackle, but the two men sitting there were regulars. A good place to fish unless foggy, then the problem is not the lack of visibility but the 'Buchan Coo'; the local name for the fog horn at the nearby Buchan Ness lighthouse. Although pointing out to sea, the horn is loud enough to deter all but the deafest of fishermen. It was not a concern today, the sun shone brightly, albeit without the warmth that comes from summer.

They sat each in their own thoughts, quite unusual for them as the conversation often flowed between the pair. Any subject could come under their scrutiny and they would discuss it at length.

The sound of the sea spilling against the rocks below, the Black Backed Gulls, Kittiwakes and a variety of other seabirds wheeling around the rocks and over the surface of the sea had Steve at peace with the world. He hadn't had a bite for over half an hour. Nothing unusual in this spot; quality over quantity was what this place was about.

"Steve, look!" Andy exclaimed suddenly breaking Steve out of his daydream. He pointed out to sea.

At first Steve couldn't see what he was showing him. Then he caught the glint of a windscreen or a wing. Two Hawker Siddeley Buccaneers were heading straight towards them low over the sea. They were so low they were level with Steve and Andy on the rock face. If they didn't gain altitude they could be the first men in history to be involved in an air accident whilst fishing. The two men watched as the aircraft approached and at the last moment pulled up to rise over the cliffs.

"Ho-leeee...!" The rest drowned out as four Rolls Royce Spey engines passed less than fifty feet over their heads.

The pair of them stood laughing with excitement.

"That first one was flown by Lieutenant Smythe, ye ken?" Steve said.

"How the hell do you know that?" Andy asked.

"I read it off his flying suit."

"Really?"

"Of course not ya muppet. I dinnae ken who's flying it."

"One of these days..." Andy said, laughing.

Steve and Andy had met two years previously at this same spot and hit it off straight away. Their friendship became stronger over the months. So it was only natural when Jane left Andy for someone else, Steve had been there to support him. He knew how difficult it was having gone through a divorce himself some years before he met Andy. Since then they had become like brothers. Now, they divided their spare time between flying, fishing, and another passion they shared: motorcycling.

"Things are not looking good at the moment," Andy said abruptly, sitting down again.

"Blue sky, fishing and a personal air show. How's that no good?"

Andy sighed, "I mean for me. Finances are a bit ropey. You know, since the divorce. I'm struggling to make ends meet."

"If you need anything let me know, anything at all. It's what mates are for."

"Cheers, Steve. I will."

They both lapsed back into silence.

Andy's rod tip suddenly shot down. "Whoa," he shouted grabbing the rod.

Five minutes later he landed himself a nice cod.

"Well, I'll be buggered," said Steve. "I've never pulled a cod like that out of here before. See, things are looking up already."

"Oh yeah. Just need to land another few thousand of these and my woes will be over," said Andy wryly.

"Is it that bad?"

"You've no idea mate," Andy said shaking his head.

"Bollocks, Andy is there nothing you can do?"

"I don't know yet, I'm working on it though."

CHAPTER THREE
13th March 1990, Jamba, Angola

President Dos Santos would have thought all his birthdays had come at once, had he been able to see the staff gathered around the table in the UNITA headquarters. A swift strike would remove the head of the UNITA beast and all his troubles would be over. Unfortunately for the President, he neither knew of the meeting, nor were his forces able to pinpoint the headquarters.

UNITA (União Nacional para a Independência Total de Angola) had once been an ally of the party now in power. In the days of the country's fight for independence from Portugal they had a common goal, to fight for a land free of foreign rule. Whilst they had a common purpose they put aside their differences. Once Angola gained its independence in 1975, the ideological differences between UNITA and the ruling party of the MPLA (Movimento Popular de Libertação de Angola) came to the fore. UNITA broadly followed the teachings of Mao, whilst the MPLA went along the Marxist route. These differences led the two sides to start a bloody civil war, one which had been raging for the past fifteen years.

The view of the UNITA leadership gradually moved away from the Maoist standpoint, declaring their sole intention was to see Angola as a country free of foreign interference.

Democracy and socialism were still at the fore, but as the ties with the United States increased, the emphasis on socialism decreased. UNITA was aligning itself with the western world. On the other hand, the Soviet Union supported the Marxist MPLA, thus a cold war by proxy situation was born.

Dr Jonas Savimbi was concerned. Once again the leaders of the western world had called for a ceasefire in Angola, and once again funding and arms from these countries was in jeopardy. He did not understand how they could not see that to win this war he needed their support. He also did not see how the world was changing and Angola's Marxist fight was no longer a priority for them. Had he seen, he would not have cared in any case. His primary concern was to free his country, and he would do whatever he could to achieve his aims.

"Gentlemen, once again we find ourselves in a corner. This month I am to meet with the Secretary of State for the United States, and I fear he will not be bringing good news."

Several of the men seated around the table nodded in agreement.

"If we are to continue our struggle and finally achieve our freedom we must have an unbroken supply of arms and food. Any threat to cut off our supplies must be circumvented. We cannot allow the whim of a foreign government to decide our fate. I have gathered you all here today to look at ways of continuing to supply our troops with the equipment and food they need. Gentlemen, please speak freely and openly. Our very survival depends on this."

He looked around the room.

General Nunda was the first to speak.

"Will this mean our normal channels for purchasing arms will no longer be open to us?"

"I fear so. We must look for alternatives. We must also look for other ways to raise funds for our struggle. South Africa will follow suit if the United States cuts us off. We will no longer be able to sell our diamonds that way."

"Who amongst our allies will remain loyal?"

"A good question, and one for which I'm afraid I do not have an answer. Perhaps Zaire will give us support. I sincerely hope so," answered Savimbi.

"When it comes to arms, we are capturing much in the way of munitions and we have obtained several of the Soviet tanks, but of course these will not be sufficient for the longer term."

General Chindondo intervened, "In that case we must find another way to sell our diamonds and purchase the arms ourselves. Could we not sell them directly? It has a twofold benefit. We cut out the middle man and we can hide the source if we are careful."

Savimbi slowly nodded. "There is much merit in your plan, Wambu. But how do we sell? None of us have any experience other than through the South Africans."

"We have control of the mines, surely it is a simple matter of having someone from one of the mines sell on our behalf?" suggested Brigadier Ukuma.

"You would have someone we don't trust take a fortune in diamonds and sell them on our behalf, are you mad?"

The Brigadier lowered his head and nodded, conceding it would probably be a mistake.

General Nunda spoke once again. "I think I may have the solution to the problem. I have a young Major under my command. He is intelligent, adaptable and is a former diamond merchant."

"Have you indeed? But can he be trusted?"

"He volunteered to join us."

"We do not have to trust him entirely. I can send one of my personal staff with him to make sure he returns with the money." General Chindondo said.

"It is an untried method. I think perhaps we should try this plan with a small number of diamonds, and if it succeeds then we can start to ship more this way," suggested General Chenda.

"Ben has a point, gentlemen," said Savimbi. "Perhaps we should try a small amount and take it from there."

Several of the men around the table murmured their agreement.

"Where is this Major now?"

"He's on a reconnaissance patrol at the moment. He's due back in a few days."

Savimbi lowered his head in thought then said, "As soon as he returns have him report to Wambu to be briefed. Do not let him know why he has to report or who he is to report to. Have someone at one of the mines prepare a selection of diamonds for our young Major to look at. If he is as good as you think, he will confirm our own assessment and the plan can go ahead. Wambu, I want you to oversee this and ensure it goes well."

CHAPTER FOUR
19th March 1990, Jamba, Angola

Major José Duarte de Oliviera Silva, Ollie to the few people he numbered as his friends, was feeling nervous. He had been summoned to the operational headquarters of UNITA, located in Jamba, UNITA's vast provisional capital of free Angola. Ollie did not like it here. Headquarters are where the bigwigs are. A summons to this place without an explanation usually meant you had done something wrong, and although he was fairly sure he had not, it was nevertheless worrying. Dr Savimbi, the leader of UNITA had been injured in February during an attack by government forces. Ollie was acutely aware that some in the party were looking for a sacrificial lamb. The attack was nothing he had any control over or responsibility for, but he knew how the system worked. Pin it on someone senior enough to have responsibility and junior enough to not be missed.

Ollie commanded a small band of soldiers under the control of General Nunda. His group operated weeks at a time in government-controlled areas gathering intelligence, the odd skirmish and occasionally carrying out sabotage. He had nothing to do with the defence of Jamba.

He sat outside an office in the underground complex that formed part of the headquarters. Jamba wasn't really a town in the conventional sense of the word, but a series of camps interlinked and spread over a hundred square kilometres. That wasn't to say it was primitive, each of the camps had hot and cold water supplies, electricity, schools, a hospital, several playing-fields, and kitchens. It was from here the bulk of the military operations of UNITA were controlled.

The air was oppressive, and he felt queasy. Ollie sat in the long dimly lit corridor wishing he had managed to get a shower before coming here, but it had been out of the question. He had just returned from a three week patrol when he received the message to present himself at the command HQ. Covered in dust, unshaven and unwashed, his uniform stuck to him, everywhere; sweat patches were visible under his arms and down his back. Hardly the state to be in when meeting someone from HQ. Though unaware of it, he was sure he did not smell too sweet either.

Ollie jumped as the door opened and a corporal announced, "The General will see you now."

The General. Shit!

The chair creaked and scraped across the wooden floor as he stood up. He marched into the office, stood to attention and saluted. He hadn't expected to see a General, but if he was to see one he would not have expected it to be this one. His knees trembled. Facing him was General Chindondo, the Chief of Intelligence.

"At ease, Major," said the General. "Please be seated. Tea?"

Ollie's face must have shown his confusion. Condemned men are not seated in the presence of a General. They stand and get bellowed at, berated, belittled, feel spittle on their face and they quake in their boots. They are then marched off to receive their punishment. They are not invited to sit and drink tea.

"Relax, Major. You're here because I need you to do me a favour."

Ollie thought for a moment. Generals do not ask for favours. Not unless they want something they shouldn't be getting. Ollie sat on the chair in front of the desk. General Chindondo indicated to the corporal he should leave the room. The General got up from behind his desk, went over to the table at the side of the room and from a china tea pot he filled two cups with the hot dark liquid.

"Milk and sugar, Major?"

"Just milk please, Sir."

The General handed him the cup and saucer, took the other and sat back behind his desk.

As hard as he tried, Ollie could not stop the trembling in his knees. He clenched them together but the cup still rattled in the saucer as he held it.

General Chindondo sipped his tea then put down the cup.

"Major, I understand you used to be in the diamond business before deciding to join us in our fight for freedom."

When his father died at the hands of the MPLA, Ollie had joined UNITA. His decision was born out of emotion. He wanted to lash out at those who had killed his father. He had no interest in politics or ideologies. Even so his mind raced. Why was the General interested in his past employment?

"Yes, Sir," he said.

The General took something from his desk drawer. He tipped out the contents of a black pouch, a considerable number of different-sized rocks tumbled out onto the table and he spread them on his blotter. Rough diamonds were never how people imagined them to be, clear and almost regular in shape. From the top drawer of his desk he took out a jeweller's loupe and placed it alongside the stones.

"Please, Major, take a look and tell me what you think."

Ollie put down his tea, picked up the loupe and put it to his eye. This was second nature to him. He carefully examined each rock in detail, which took some considerable time. Finally he put down the loupe and separated two of the diamonds from the rest. He then sat back in his chair and looked at the General.

"Well?" asked the General.

"Very impressive, Sir," said Ollie.

"So tell me what did you see?"

"These are stones of exceptional quality, Sir. They are almost colourless and they have few inclusions in them. Not one of these is less than five carats I would think."

"And the value, Major?"

"Without access to up to date information on the diamond market that's hard to say, but I would imagine on the open market somewhere in the region of five to six million dollars, Sir."

"And this one?" The General pointed to one of the two separated stones.

"An outstanding specimen, Sir. It appears to be internally flawless and is a good colour. I would think that alone would bring quarter of a million."

Picking up the remaining stone the General said, "What about this one?"

"I hope you are not being serious, Sir." Ollie shook his head.

The General laughed and tossed the final stone into his waste basket. He leaned back in his chair and steepled his fingers.

"Major," he paused for a moment, "what I am going to tell you must not be discussed with anyone outside this office."

Ollie nodded.

"We are on the verge of agreeing another ceasefire with the MPLA. There's a lot of international pressure to bring this conflict to an end. A significant amount of our funding comes from the United States. There are concerns within the party that once we do have a ceasefire, these funds will dry up. Whilst a ceasefire is most agreeable, there are those who do not think it will last. We must still be in a position to fight again if that is the case. We control much of the diamond mining now, so we are able to fund our quest for independence. The problem is we're finding it harder to sell our diamonds on the open market. More and more, the origin is being questioned. We want you to sell these diamonds for cash, and as quickly as is reasonably possible. We realise the amount from this sale will be a small part of our requirements, but we have to achieve what we can, where we can. If this is successful, we will make more sales this way. Think of this as a small experiment. I assume you still have contacts in the industry who could arrange this?"

"It has been a while, but I am sure I will be able to find someone who would not ask too many questions, Sir."

"Good. We accept it will take some time. You have three months to arrange this. We are willing to accept considerably less than the open market value to ensure we have a quick sale, but please, do not disclose the funds will be coming to us. Discretion is absolutely vital. You can accept as little as two million dollars, but obviously the more you can obtain, the better. Will you need to be there in person to sell them?"

"Yes, Sir. It would be better that way."

The General handed an envelope to Ollie.

"This is a letter of authority signed by myself. Use it to obtain anything you need — within reason."

He picked up the phone on his desk and waited for a few moments.

"Please send in Lieutenant Pereira."

A neat-cut officer entered the room and stood to attention. It was the same Lieutenant who had collected Ollie on his return from the patrol.

"One final thing, Major, you will be accompanied by Lieutenant Pereira. He is on my personal staff. He will carry the diamonds for you on your trip and he will carry the money on your return. He will ensure both the diamonds and money are safe."

The message was clear. The General may have chosen him for this mission because of his experience in the diamond trade, but Ollie was clearly not to be trusted to leave the country alone with a fortune in diamonds, or to return with a fortune in cash. He hoped nothing would go wrong.

"Now if you will excuse me, Major, I have some important business to attend to, and I'm sure you would like to make a start on our little operation."

"Yes, Sir", Ollie saluted and followed the Lieutenant out of the room.

"Sir?" the Lieutenant said. "This way please, Sir. The General has put a small office at our disposal."

The Lieutenant escorted Ollie along the corridor to a tiny office.

Ollie stood in the doorway and glanced around the room. It was little more than a large cupboard.

"This is it?" he asked. It was furnished with two desks and three chairs, none of them matching. A telephone sat on one of the desks and a half-filled waste basket was by the door. The sole concession to air conditioning was the large fan in the corner.

"Yes, Sir," replied the Lieutenant.

Ollie shrugged his shoulders. At least he was away from tents, mosquitoes and bullets.

CHAPTER FIVE
19th March 1990, North Atlantic

'United States of America' reflected in the highly-polished engine cowling. Should anyone be unsure of the origin and importance of this aircraft, then the Presidential seal painted on the nose would remove all doubt. However, this was not Air Force One; the President was not on board, but the fact it was one of the Presidential aircraft bore testament to the importance of the person it was carrying.

Seated at a desk in the cabin, Secretary of State, James Baker, was deep in thought at the contents of the paper he was studying. He was on his way to the ceremony to celebrate the official independence of the African State of Namibia. The world was changing. Last year the Berlin Wall had fallen, and Germany was finally going to be reunited. The Soviet stranglehold on the eastern bloc countries was rapidly diminishing. The cold war was coming to an end. Independence for Namibia was a part of that global change. In Angola, Cuban troops had been pulled back from the Namibian border. That had been part of the deal for independence. The Cubans were supporting the Marxist government MPLA, against the anti-communist UNITA. Secretary Baker was reading the latest analysis of the political situation. The time was ripe for pressure to be applied to both sides and bring this war to an end. There was a chance that stability could be brought to the region and that was worth pursuing, but if either side in Angola thought they had an advantage, they would continue the conflict. Although he was to convey the message to UNITA that the covert financial support would continue, he was to leave them under no illusions the support would be withdrawn once the government accepted UNITA represented a significant number of Angolans. However, the Angolan situation was not that simple. Even though the cold war was diminishing, this was still a part of it, with the Soviets supporting the Cubans. As was often the case, Potomac politics were inextricably entwined, with many of the Washington Democrats seeing the continued support for UNITA as being driven entirely by Republican politics. To the right wing Republicans, the Bush administration had sold out everywhere, and the Democrats felt the response of the administration was to hang tough on Angola to appease the right wingers.

The nineteen-hour flight from Washington had been punctuated by two fuel stops, one in Cayenne, French Guiana and one on Ascension Island. At the start of the flight there had been some unexpected entertainment on board. World famous jazz trumpeter Dizzy Gillespie had been invited by the government of Namibia to play at the independence celebrations and Secretary Baker had invited him along as a guest on the flight. Dizzy had treated them all to an impromptu concert on board the Presidential aircraft, and it had made an entertaining change from the usual workload before retiring to bed.

Now, Secretary Baker was reading his last briefing paper before arriving in the newly independent country. He had meetings scheduled with several people over the next few days, in several countries. Before those meetings, Secretary Baker intended to meet Eduard Shevardnadze, his opposite number in the Soviet Union. This bloody civil war had to be halted. It was costing lives, and it was costing the US and Soviet taxpayers. Secretary Baker knew this was going to be a busy week, but when had he not had a busy week?

CHAPTER SIX

19th March 1990, Jamba, Angola

Born and raised in Saurimo, the provincial capital of the Lunda Sul region of Angola, Ollie had been around diamonds all his life. His Portuguese father had been a senior figure at one of the numerous small diamond mines in the region, and Ollie grew up with diamonds in his blood. His father made sure when Ollie started work at the mine he started from the bottom, literally. He knew what the conditions were like for the miners and he appreciated the dangers they faced every day, bringing the precious rocks to the surface. It was the only way to understand diamonds, he had told Ollie.

He went on to learn all aspects of mining, grading and selling diamonds. He was a particularly skilled negotiator when it came to selling on the open market. That was the position he held before he joined UNITA, and now it seemed he would be a negotiator again.

Ollie's mother was of Chokwe descent. She died of natural causes shortly after his birth; their Lunda-Chokwe housekeeper becoming Ollie's surrogate mother. His skin was dark and his features more African than European. He could easily hide the fact he was Mestiço, a mixed race Angolan. That proved useful in UNITA where there existed a strong mistrust of the Portuguese and Mestiço. Understandable, as the Angolans had only recently gained their independence from the Portuguese.

Ollie knew deep down he did not really want to fight. He had wanted to punish the people who killed his father. Even when doing something he didn't want to do, it was typical of him to carry it out to the best of his ability. His quick and decisive thinking, as well as an ability to plan on the move, brought him to the attention of his superiors and he rapidly gained promotion. It wasn't long before he attained the rank of Major and took command of a unit of troops specialising in long range patrols, where his talent for thinking on his feet was put to good use.

Now he was going to have to use that ability for something else. This trip must be turned to his advantage and get him out of Angola, permanently; not to mention the considerable amount of money the diamonds would bring. Ollie had never stolen anything in his life, but this wasn't about the money. It was about surviving. Yes, he would be wealthy, but more importantly he would be alive. There was nothing here for him now; his desire for revenge had been replaced with sadness.

Lieutenant Pereira was the stumbling block to Ollie's plans. He would have the diamonds with him at all times, except when they would be with the buyers, and Pereira would still be present watching like a hawk. Ollie smiled; the Lieutenant had quite a prominent beak. There had to be a way of getting the diamonds away from him.

He briefly flirted with the idea of offering a bribe to Pereira but dismissed it straight away. Anyone on General

Chindondo's personal staff was highly unlikely to be open to bribes. Still, six million dollars was a lot of money, but he couldn't take the chance the Lieutenant would report him. Dr Savimbi did not like people who crossed him. No, this had to be something that would allow him to vanish with the diamonds before anyone got a hint of what he was planning. He wanted to vanish alive, not in some unmarked grave in Angola.

He thought hard of ways he could take the diamonds and run, but he could not come up with a way to get the Lieutenant out of the picture. If he solved the problem of Pereira then he would need to dispose of the diamonds. He would set up a legitimate deal with a buyer; he needed to do that to keep the Lieutenant happy anyway; then if he managed to get away with the stones, he would sell to someone else, allowing the trail to go cold.

Ollie's preference was to trade with the London dealers. He knew there were a few who were crooked but the majority were genuine and could be trusted, as he was sure they were elsewhere, but he was used to the London market. Sure, they would squeeze the last dollar out of the deal, but that was what negotiation was about.

He already had someone in mind he would approach to set up the legitimate deal, providing the name was on the list. As for the other part of the plan, he knew a few who were on the fringes of the business. The trick was going to be setting up a plan and an escape without Pereira getting wind of it. He would have to tread carefully indeed.

The door opened suddenly and Pereira entered carrying a tray with cups, a kettle, and a box of tea.

"Now that's a good start," Ollie said. "I've had one decent cup of tea since the beginning of the last patrol, and I didn't get to finish that. You appeared and whisked me away."

"Sorry, Sir. I can't promise my tea will be any good."

"It can't be any worse than on patrol. I can live with that for the time being."

"We're getting a list of dealers faxed here soon Sir."

"Thank you. In the meantime, get that kettle working, Lieutenant. I'm absolutely parched."

Ollie's mind drifted back to the problem of getting his hands on the diamonds. The trip to London would be interesting.

Of one thing he was sure, he would not be returning to Angola.

CHAPTER SEVEN
20th March 1990, Windhoek, Namibia

"Eduard, so good to see you again."

Secretary Baker stretched out his hand to his Russian counterpart. The greeting was warm and genuine.

"James, my friend, how are you keeping?"

"I would like to stay still for five minutes, Eduard."

Shevardnadze let out a laugh. "You love it James, all this jetting around. You enjoy the cut and thrust of diplomacy too. We both do, otherwise why would be in politics?"

Secretary Baker joined in the laughter.

"You know, you may well be right."

"Of course I'm right, I'm Russian. We are never wrong my friend!"

"On that I'm afraid we will have to agree to disagree."

"But of course my dear James, otherwise you would be Russian too. No?"

The laughter continued as they took up their seats.

The residence of the US Ambassador had been chosen as the venue for the meeting: a striking building situated in the Eros district of Windhoek. Although the US Embassy was opening on the same day as Namibia gained its independence, an Ambassador had yet to be appointed, which gave the two men ample opportunity to meet in private, on both an official and unofficial level.

"Eduard, before we get down to the official business, there is a little matter I would like to discuss first."

"Of course James, of course."

"Angola."

Shevardnadze threw up his hands and nodded. "Ah, the ever present thorn in our sides. What do you have in mind?"

Both the Soviet Union and the United States were heavily involved in the civil war in Angola. As was to be expected, they were on opposite sides. Although not directly involved in the fighting, they were supplying arms by various means and advisors to the troops involved. Soviet-backed Cuba had troops in Angola to support the government. South Africa and Zaire had gone in on the side of UNITA with support of the United States. As is usual in any sort of multi-national conflict, the dynamics of the situation were extremely complex.

"I want us to be on the same page when we meet Dos Santos and Savimbi." Senator Baker emphasised his words with both hands. "I suggest we lay it on the line to them about the ceasefire talks. They're full of promises, and as soon as our backs are turned they are back to squabbling like school children. Unfortunately, they're school children with guns. We must get the message across to them; make it work, or the money stops."

"And you want me to deliver this message too?"

Secretary Baker nodded.

"Well, I must say, off the record, it's costing the Soviet Union a fortune."

This brought a smile to Secretary Baker's face. They had quite a few 'off the record' talks, such was the trust between these two men. A far cry from the old days of 'keep everything secret at all costs' diplomacy. He was also glad to hear the Soviets considering the financial aspects of the conflict, and not only the ideologies involved.

Their first meeting had been the previous March and this would be the seventh since then. Whilst the initial encounters had been the typically stilted East-West diplomacy type affairs, genuine warmth had developed between the two diplomats and they were well on the way to becoming firm friends. Although their ideologies were poles apart, their humanity was not. They both had a genuine desire to see peace in the world.

"I thought you might see it that way, Eduard. So I can count on you delivering the same message?"

The Soviet minister threw up his hands again in a gesture of acceptance.

"But of course my friend. We have no desire to see this conflict continue any more than you do."

Secretary Baker smiled.

"I thought that would be the case. We must try to stop this bloodshed," he paused. "Anyway, before we get down to government business, how is Nanuli keeping?"

CHAPTER EIGHT
2nd April 1990, Jamba, Angola

Once again, Ollie found himself being ushered in to see General Chindondo. This time he felt more at ease. He now worked for the General. Ollie had nothing to fear as long as he did his best for him, and he knew he was good at his job.

"Major, please take a seat. Please, bring me up to date with your preparations."

Ollie sat in the same chair in front of the General's desk. This time however there was no offer of tea.

"Yes, Sir. I have identified two dealers I believe will be suitable for this operation. We are preparing photographs of the diamonds to send by fax and although they will be black and white they will have to suffice. In any case, any dealer worth his salt will need to examine them in person before making any sort of commitment to buy."

The General nodded.

Ollie continued. "Once the photographs and details have been faxed we will wait to see whether these two men are interested in pursuing it any further. I have had some previous contact with both of them. Neither gives me any cause for concern regarding this deal. If they are interested, our intention is to fly from Lusaka directly to London."

"Why London, Major?"

"I've mainly done business with the London dealers. I'm familiar with their methods, and I believe I can obtain a better price there than in Amsterdam. I also believe the London merchants are less likely to ask awkward questions."

General Chindondo pursed his lips then asked, "Are they trustworthy?"

"Most of them are, Sir. There are some I would not trust of course, but neither would I deal with them. These two I believe will be discreet and can be trusted. As with all walks of life there are those you can trust and those you cannot."

"Indeed, Major." He paused for a few seconds. "Last time we spoke I suggested there were some who believed the Americans were about to change their stance on helping our cause."

Ollie nodded.

"It would seem that is no longer supposition, Major. It was made clear to Dr Savimbi in a meeting with the American Secretary of State that patience and money are running out. My understanding is the Soviets have indicated the same to the government leaders. It is now vital we find a reliable way to sell our diamonds independent of the South African route. There is a good opportunity for us to gain the upper hand here and we must not waste it."

"I understand, Sir. I will ensure we get the best possible deal. You must appreciate however, if we flood the market with high-quality diamonds we will bring the price down."

"Then we will have to sell even more to make up for the shortfall."

"Sir, it doesn't work like..."

The General held up his hand and silenced Ollie.

"I am fully aware of how the market works, my dear Major. I am passing on the words of our leader."

Ollie sighed, "Yes of course, Sir. I understand."

General Chindondo smiled.

"General Nunda speaks highly of you. He believes you are very smart. I can see why he would say that, Major. A wise man knows when to stay silent."

Ollie smiled.

The General rose from behind his desk and gestured towards the door.

As he accompanied Ollie, he put his hand on the Major's shoulder.

"Dr Savimbi is taking a personal interest in this operation. I'm sure your success will be rewarded when the time comes, Major."

As Ollie returned to his office, he reflected on the fact the General had not mentioned anything about the consequences of failure. If some of the rumours he had heard were true about those who had displeased Dr Savimbi, he already knew the answer.

CHAPTER NINE
2nd April 1990, Jamba, Angola

Lieutenant Pereira was not a complicated man. As far as he was concerned his membership of UNITA stemmed from his belief in the cause. He did not question what they were doing because what they were doing must be right. He would carry out whatever orders he was given.

The General had given him a straight-forward task. Look after the diamonds on the way there, and the money on the way back. He understood it to mean the Major was not to be trusted, and rightly so in his opinion. He couldn't put his finger on it but something wasn't quite right about the Major. He was too nice, too open. He must be hiding something.

Pereira knew little about the diamond trade, so the Major would certainly have to lead in that respect, but when it came to guarding things, Pereira knew his job.

Whilst the Major was away briefing the General, he took the opportunity to have a poke around in the Major's desk drawers. He was disappointed to find nothing to indicate the Major was anything other than what he appeared to be. He discovered no secret books or incriminating pieces of paper. In fact the Major appeared to be a meticulously organised officer.

This worried Pereira. His instincts were rarely wrong. He would keep a close eye on his charge.

The journey to London filled him with both excitement and fear. He had never been to the Angolan capital let alone outside the country. Nor had he ever been in an aeroplane. He wished he could try that first before embarking on a flight that would be in excess of ten hours. What if he didn't like it?

On the other hand an opportunity to see the outside world was something had never considered, and now it was about to happen.

He wanted nothing to go wrong with this operation. He liked to please the General, and one day he would gain his promotion. He had a feeling this was to be the first step to better things for him.

CHAPTER TEN

4th April 1990, Hatton Garden, London

The Hatton Garden district of London was once a grand residential area, but by the late nineteenth century, the diamond industry had become firmly established. Some eight hundred businesses now occupied Hatton Gardens and the surrounding streets: not all involved in the diamond trade, but nearly all connected to the jewellery business in some way.

Harry Hart occupied a small office on the top floor of a three-storey red-brick building in Hatton Wall, a narrow street connecting Hatton Gardens with Leather Street. It was flanked on either side by more three- and four-storey buildings, and like Harry's, most had seen better days, with peeling paintwork and crumbling brickwork. A pawnbroker occupied the ground floor, which seemed at odds with the brightly lit jewellery shops in the adjacent Hatton Gardens. Still, this was London; fortunes were both made and lost in the City. Pawnbrokers and diamond merchants each had a role to play.

The seediness of the building suited Harry. The office he occupied continued the run-down theme. A door sporting opaque, reeded glass, with H & H Associates emblazoned in peeling gold shadow letters, announced to the customer they had finally made it after the climb up the steep and narrow staircase.

There were no actual associates, but Harry found the suggestion of others involved in his business to be useful in his negotiations.

Yellowing paint that perhaps had once been brilliant white covered the walls. The carpet would have been more at home in a cheap nineteen-seventies' restaurant, and quite possibly may have come from one. A grey metal filing cabinet clashed with the polished mahogany desk, and a cheap black leather office chair. His clients were rewarded with a rather grand wing-back brown leather armchair, which would not have looked out of place in a stately home, but was at odds with the current setting. Dusty piles of old trade magazines were stacked everywhere and a small safe occupied one corner.

His regular clients knew whilst the building and offices gave the impression of decay, nothing could be further from the truth about Harry. He was in the business of buying and selling diamonds, both the rough and the cut variety.

Harry was slim and stood 6'4" tall, topped off with neatly combed dark hair, parted to one side. A pair of large black rimmed glasses perched on his nose. Since the Superman movie he had become known as 'Clark' to his few friends because of his uncanny resemblance to the superhero's alter ego. Not that Harry minded much. He used the image well, even down to copying the habit of pushing his glasses back up his nose. It gave him an air of vulnerability that more than one trader found to his cost, was only a veneer.

A third-generation immigrant from Belgium, Harry's family name had originally been Hardt. His grandfather changed it to Hart when they moved to England in 1936. Aware of the rise of the Nazis, and certain that Europe would fall to the Third Reich; his grandfather moved the entire family out of Belgium. Many of his compatriots thought he was wrong, and chose to stay, sadly paying with their lives when the Nazis decimated the Jewish population of Antwerp, where Harry's grandfather traded in diamonds. After moving, his grandfather continued in his trade until the outbreak of the war, when he volunteered to act as a buyer for the British government, switching to buying industrial diamonds, much needed for the war effort.

Once the war ended he returned to his old business of buying and selling diamonds for jewellery. Harry's father, Harald, joined the business as soon as he was old enough, and at the age of sixteen so did Harry. Harry grew up with diamonds; he had a good grasp of the basics of the trade, by the age of eight. Now Harry worked alone, his father had passed away some years ago.

His deep knowledge of the diamond industry earned him a lot of respect in the business. He was known to be a hard but fair man to bargain with. When you bought diamonds from Harry, you were certain you were getting quality. When you sold diamonds to him, you would get a fair price. Woe betide anyone trying to pull the wool over Harry's eyes. His many contacts meant you would be unlikely to sell to any of the other legitimate dealers in London, once it was known Harry wouldn't deal with you. Your selling would have to be done on the fringes, and you would be ripped off on every deal.

Harry's phone rang.

"H and H. Harry Hart speaking."

"Good afternoon Mr Hart," said the voice at the other end.

The line was not very clear but Harry could just about make out what was being said.

"My name is Ollie Silva. I believe I may have had some dealings in the past with you..."

"Oll..!" Harry started to say.

Ollie continued speaking, "...and I wondered if you would be interested in buying some diamonds I have for sale?"

Harry paused. "That does rather depend Mr Silva. What kind of diamonds are we talking about, value, quality, etcetera?"

"These are top quality uncut, approximately one thousand carats, D to F and mainly VVS1. All are stones and we have one of exceptional quality. We are looking for something in the region of two and a half to three million dollars which, I hasten to add, is far below market value. We will need payment in cash."

Harry let out a slow, silent whistle. Diamonds classified as stone crystalline structure had the highest yield when cut. Almost fifty percent of the original would be retained after cutting. The colour and inclusions were good too. As long as the actual items matched their description, then these were indeed high quality and high value.

"And may I ask the origin?"

"Oh you may ask Mr Hart, just don't expect an answer," said Ollie.

Harry was aware many of the diamond producing countries of the world also happened to be where there was civil unrest, or outright war. Most, if not all of these countries were in central and southern Africa. Rebel forces often obtained diamonds to fund their hostilities with the established government. These diamonds came from some of the best areas for quality, and often sold at a price well below their worth to make for a quick sale.

Harry realised the value of these particular diamonds was beyond his immediate resources, though there were people in London he could contact who would be prepared to shell out for diamonds of dubious origin in order to make a fast buck. He also knew if these diamonds were as good as suggested then he was likely to make quite a killing on them. An unfortunate turn of phrase given their likely origin. A smile flickered across Harry's face at his own pun.

"I take it there is room for negotiation here?" asked Harry.

"There is always room for some negotiation," said Ollie.

"I am going to have to speak with a few people about this," said Harry. "Is there a number I can get back to you on?"

"How long do you need to contact these few people, Mr Hart?"

"At least a couple of weeks to get the right ones. Those who are not going to insist on the answer to the origin question. I'll need some photographs, especially of any specimen pieces, and a comprehensive list of all the diamonds. I am sure you know what to provide, Mr Silva."

"Indeed I do, Mr Hart, and it is understandable. Let me have your fax number and I will fax the photographs and list as soon as I can, and I will of course send the original photographs by mail. They may take considerably longer to get to you."

Harry gave him the number.

"I will call you back in three weeks. We need to make sure we have the right deal. Lives may depend on it. Goodbye, Mr Hart."

CHAPTER ELEVEN
4th April 1990, Aberdeen, Scotland

Andy opened the door to his house and his heart sank: another pile of letters behind the door. He dropped his rucksack in the hall, hung up his coat and picked up the stack of mail.

Ever since Jane walked out of his life he had struggled with the huge pile of debt she left behind. She had run up their credit cards to the maximum, the month before she left him for another man; one she expected to keep her in the manner she thought she deserved; a fact that only came to light when Andy received the bills the following month. She and her new man disappeared shortly afterwards. Despite her being jointly responsible for their debt, he had little hope of her ever paying. Not for the first time, he wondered what he had done to her to deserve this.

He went to the kitchen and filled the kettle. "When in trouble make a cuppa," his mother had always said to him. He doubted the whole of Tetley's could solve this problem.

Where did it all go wrong? As far as he was concerned the marriage had been a happy one. Shift-work puts a strain on any relationship but he had been unaware of anything to indicate their marriage was in trouble. They were like any other married couple with their normal ups and downs.

Unfortunately, and unknown to him, she had always harboured a taste for the finer things in life and her head had been turned by someone who could offer that. How they met, Andy had no idea, and Jane wouldn't say; but it was clear she wanted more than Andy could give her. Not only that, but it appeared she wanted him to suffer because he could not supply those things. And boy was he suffering.

He finally steeled himself to open the new batch of letters. They did not make for good reading. The patience of the credit card companies had finally run out. To be fair, they had been patient with him so far, but his wage did not cover the minimum payments, the mortgage and living expenses. It didn't matter how many times he rearranged the figures, there was more going out than coming in. He could make some small savings here and there, but even when they were factored in, the end figure was still a minus. They had relied on Jane's income to make ends meet. Andy had considered selling the house, but of all the places he had chosen to buy, this area had a stalled market. New builds were all around and they were the ones selling. Nobody wanted a house that was ten years old; brand new or old dominated the market, the in-betweens weren't selling. His neighbour's house had been on the market for nine months, and was still unsold. What chance did he have of selling in time to satisfy his creditors?

He finished making the cup of tea, returned with a steaming mug and sat at the dining table again, staring at the one remaining envelope. He didn't want to open it, scared of what he would find inside. How did others cope with debt like this he wondered? What did they do to stop the churning inside, the feeling of being cornered without a way out? Well, not a way he would contemplate anyway. How many people took their lives as the ultimate means of avoiding this sense of total and utter helplessness?

He opened the final letter and fell into absolute despair; he wanted to be physically sick. The house would be repossessed. The mortgage company was not prepared to accept his repayment proposal, and unless he cleared the arrears in the next fourteen days they would start proceedings to repossess the property. Well, wasn't that the icing on the cake?

Andy dropped his head into his hands. It would take some sort of miracle to sort out this mess. He felt like a trapped animal. He was cornered with no means of escape. Really, what had he done to deserve this?

CHAPTER TWELVE

4th April 1990, Wapping, London

At first glance Donald Munro could be mistaken for a city banker, a lawyer, or a politician in his immaculately pressed, pin-striped, three-piece suit, and handmade Italian shoes. The dark, wavy hair was always neatly groomed and his hands freshly manicured. Donald would not have looked out of place at any Kensington dinner party. He was none of those. He was a crook.

His Glasgow accent, which remained strong despite his many years in London, made him seem even more menacing. Donald was proud of his roots and had no intention of losing his accent, although the language he used was more Conan-Doyle than Rabbie Burns, the accent was unmistakable.

He had grown up in the Maryhill district of Glasgow in the nineteen-fifties. Maryhill was not the best place to be for a quiet life in the nineteen-fifties. For a short while he ran with a gang headed by a man who later became known as the Glasgow Godfather. Although Donald was grateful for the chance to be with the gang, he soon realised his future lay with his own gang, doing things his way. Not wanting to antagonise his mentor, he explained his plans to him, and left Glasgow with his blessings. He was nineteen when he moved to London.

He arrived in the East End, as the reign of the notorious Kray twins came to an end. He was able to step into part of the vacuum left by their departure, and carve out a niche for himself. Carve was appropriate. Like many Glaswegian criminals of that era, Donald was adept in the use of the open razor. No one was going to step on his toes and get away with it. His methods of protecting himself, and the way he dealt with others wanting to try their luck on his turf, earned a fearsome reputation by the age of twenty-five.

His short apprenticeship in Glasgow taught him a great deal. Like his mentor, he was able to plan his crimes well. He weighed up all the possible outcomes of a particular scenario and made sure contingency plans were in place for each and every one of them. This meticulous attention to detail led to some high profile crimes being committed, with the police not having an inkling of Donald's involvement.

There were few things he would not turn his hand to, in order to make money. The only thing out of bounds was kids. He had kids of his own and would not tolerate anyone using them in any way.

Donald was wise beyond his years when he moved south. He needed a front that would keep him out of the clutches of the law. His visible success was in a business buying and selling gem stones, mainly diamonds. As he had started his career in the East End, he shunned the Hatton Garden district, preferring to work from his offices in Wapping High Street, close to where he started. Rumours abounded of competitors who disappeared without a trace and his involvement in organised crime, but he laughed it off telling people these rumours always followed those who were successful.

Several people crossed Donald and did indeed meet an untimely end in the River Thames, so it was ironic his offices were a stone's throw from the Headquarters of the Thames River Police. The gemstone business served as a useful tool for laundering money for his not so legitimate enterprises. Now in his early forties he was quite a wealthy man, but he was always on the lookout to make more money, legitimately or otherwise.

Anyone entering Donald's offices would be forgiven for thinking they had stepped into an eighteenth-century mansion. The furnishings were not reproduction pieces. Donald appreciated beauty and craftsmanship and he was happy to invest his money in decorating his offices. After all, he spent most of his time there. The only concession to the modern world was the gymnasium in the room adjacent to his office. He had no intention of being deposed from his top spot through being unfit, and he worked out every day with his personal trainer.

Seated at an authentic Chippendale desk looking over figures from his legitimate business, Donald frowned when there was a knock at the door. He hated to be interrupted when working.

"Come."

"Some guy called Hart on the phone, Mr Munro. I told him you were busy, but he says it's important. Something to do with diamonds at a knockdown price."

Lenny was one of Donald's inner circle of trusted men. He didn't call them bodyguards but they were. Donald might still be tasty with a razor, but a razor always lost against a gun. Donald's men were well-armed and loyal. At least he hoped they were loyal. They ought to be, they were well paid.

Lenny was handy with a gun and no mean street fighter. Unfortunately nature appeared to have been unkind to him when it came to mental agility. Even reading a comic could be a struggle for him at times. For Donald that was not a bad thing. Bright people had bright ideas. He didn't want anyone thinking about taking over the top slot.

"Did ye happen to get a first name by any chance Lenny?"

"Oh yeah, Harry."

Donald knew of Harry Hart of course. He was a dealer with a reputation for being fair and absolutely above board. Why on earth would he be calling him?

"Okay put him through."

"If you say so, Mr Munro."

"I thought I just did."

Lenny frowned and went back to the outer office. Donald knew he was trying to work out the last exchange of words.

The phone rang on Donald's desk.

"Good morning, Mr Hart. To what do we owe this pleasure?" Although Donald was proud of his heritage he realised many in the city could not understand his strong accent. His telephone voice was the Queen's English, spoken with only a slightly diluted Maryhill accent.

"Mr Munro, good morning. I have something that may be of interest to you, and could make us both a lot of money."

"Have you indeed, Mr Hart? Please go on."

Harry explained what was on offer and the potential profit.

"So why me, Mr Hart? I'm sure there are plenty of other...ah...merchants you could approach."

"Because these diamonds are from a source that doesn't want any questions asked about their origin — if you get my drift. I know you are a man of discretion, Mr Munro."

"Indeed I am, Mr Hart, indeed I am. If what you are telling me is true, then it is possible we could come to some arrangement. Perhaps we should meet to discuss it further."

"Glad you see it that way, Mr Munro. May I suggest we meet on board the Tattershall Castle, Victoria Embankment? I know it's a bit of a trek for you, but it's away from the prying eyes of people who may know us. Is three o'clock this afternoon convenient?"

"That's fine."

"Three o'clock it is then."

"Just one small thing," Donald paused, "as far as I'm aware we've never met. How will I know you?"

"Keep a look out for Superman."

"Superman, Mr Hart?"

"Trust me; you will know it's me."

"If you say so, Mr Hart." Donald hung up.

"Lenny," he called to the next room.

Lenny came into the room, "Yes, Mr Munro?"

"Get Willie to find out all he can about Harry Hart, of H and H Diamonds, and get yourself ready to go out. We're going to meet Superman."

Donald was amused by the look of puzzlement on Lenny's face as he left. He shook his head, he really shouldn't tease the man like that, but Donald had always been a bit of a leg puller.

He was still curious as to why Harry Hart had approached him of all people. From all he had heard, Hart was squeaky clean, and he was sure he must be aware of Donald's own reputation, however well he explained it away. There must be other merchants who would deal without asking questions, so why him? He would keep a close eye on Hart. Not that he had anything concrete to worry about, but being suspicious about everyone and everything had kept him alive and out of prison so far.

CHAPTER THIRTEEN
4th April 1990, Victoria Embankment, London

Victoria Embankment is a leafy avenue which accompanies the River Thames on part of its journey through central London. The river walk was filled with throngs of tourists, intent on taking photographs and the adjacent road packed with buses, taxis and cars. It was here the paddle steamer, Tattershall Castle was moored. A passenger ferry in a former life, she was now permanently moored a few hundred yards from the seat of government. A new lease of life as a bar, restaurant and night club suited her well.

Donald Munro sat at one of the several tables on the top deck, his glass empty. At one time, Donald would have been on the hard stuff, even at this time of day. For the past eighteen years the only alcohol that passed his lips had been champagne on special occasions. He wasn't against alcohol, but it dimmed his mind a little too much. He liked to be sharp.

From his seat he had a good view of the gangplank onto the ship. He liked the idea of calling it a gangplank. It conjured up images of pirates and treasure. Donald was sure had he been alive in the eighteenth century he would have been a pirate. He thought of himself as someone who took advantage whenever he could, fair or unfair. Captain Munro, scourge of the high seas. He liked that. Maybe in those days they would not have had gangplanks so wide, nor would they be covered, so perhaps he should think of this one as more of a walkway.

Lenny stood nearby, leaning against the rail, doing his best to blend into the background — and failing miserably.

Donald watched as a tall man in a suit came down the walkway. He was carrying an A4 manila folder. Clark Kent. Now he knew what Hart had meant when he said to watch out for Superman. The man stopped at the bottom of the walkway, looked around the deck and pushed his glasses back up his nose. Donald waved him over.

"Mr Hart?"

"Mr Munro I presume."

"Indeed Mr Hart, indeed. Please, call me Donald." He offered his hand to Harry.

"Clark, for obvious reasons," said Harry, noting the firmness of the handshake.

Donald laughed. "You did have me wondering how we were going to make this meeting discreet, with you dressed in a red cape, and a blue suit."

Harry smiled.

"Drink, Clark?"

"Thank you, I'll have a gin and tonic."

Donald signalled to Lenny to come over.

"A gin and tonic for Mr Hart and Perrier for myself, if you would please, Lenny."

"Certainly, Mr Munro."

"Handy to have around, but not the brightest," Donald said when Lenny had gone below to get the drinks from the bar.

Harry raised his eyebrows. There wasn't really much he could say.

"So Clark, let's get down to business. First of all why me?"

"As I said on the phone, I know you can be discreet. The seller has asked me to find someone who is not going to ask too many questions. I don't know for sure, but I believe these diamonds are going to be used to fund a rebel army. Too many of the dealers I know would want to ask questions."

"How do you know how good they are?"

"I don't for sure. I only have a description of the larger pieces and photographs. If they live up to expectations, then we should do quite well out of them."

Lenny returned with the drinks and set them down on the table. Donald motioned for him to take up his position leaning against the rail and failing to blend in again.

"No sense in too many people knowing about this," he said to Harry. "I do have to say from the description you gave they do seem to be high quality."

Harry opened the folder and pulled out several 10" x 8" photographs and laid them in front of Donald.

Donald studied them for a few minutes. "It's impossible to tell from the photographs if they're genuine, but assuming they are, and if they are of the quality you say, I do see some merit in this deal. Who else have you asked?"

"No one yet. Mr...err...Donald"

"How much?"

"Three million dollars."

Munro paused for a few seconds. "Could you raise half?"

"Not in the time we have available. I could if I sell some of my stock, but that would take time. I could maybe raise five hundred thousand in cash, but no more than that."

Donald paused. "I'm not sure I want anyone else to know about this."

"I could possibly get the rest by the beginning of July, but not before. The seller wants a sale as quickly as possible."

"How about you let me have the half a million: I'll fund the rest of the deal, you then pay me the balance of what you owe, at the beginning of July?" suggested Donald.

"That means you take all the risk. Hardly seems fair."

"Indeed, Clark. That is why I propose to take eighty percent of the profits."

Clark choked on his drink. "I think that's a little steep. Even if you are taking the lion's share of the risk I'm the one who has the deal. How about sixty-forty?"

Donald laughed. "I heard you drive a hard bargain Clark. If you're ever in need of employment I am sure I could find a position for you. Seventy-thirty."

Harry mulled it over for a moment then stuck out his hand. "Deal."

The sudden movement made Lenny step forward and reach into his jacket. Donald waved him away as he shook Harry's hand.

"So what's the next step?"

"The seller is calling me back next week. We'll set up a meeting and see if they're as good as he says they are. If all is well we hand over the cash, and he hands over the diamonds."

"It sounds like a plan to me," said Munro.

He reached out to shake Harry's hand again. As he did so, he looked him in the eye and said, "I hope this goes well, Clark, I really do."

So did Harry.

CHAPTER FOURTEEN
4th April 1990, Embankment, London

Harry left the Tattershall Castle and walked to Embankment tube station. Once inside he leaned against a wall and closed his eyes for a moment. He felt like the mouse that had evaded the cat. His heart was racing, his brow was wet and he felt totally wrung out. He had known Munro was a dodgy character, but now he knew for certain if this went wrong, he would probably end up as part of the foundation for a new flyover, or inspecting the animal life at the bottom of the Thames. Heaven knows what they would do to him before that happened.

He headed back to his office, taking the Circle Line to Farringdon. It wasn't the nearest tube station, nor the most direct route, but at least he could sit for a few minutes and pull himself together again, give himself time to think. The tube was busy, but not yet packed with the sticky, sweaty bodies of commuters heading back to their private lives; only to repeat the performance the next day. Harry could set his own hours and travel when he wanted to; something to be thankful for. He wasn't a religious person, but as far as he was concerned, Hell must be similar to a tube train at rush hour.

He took the stairs two at a time to the station exit and found he felt a little more composed. If anything he was feeling elated. He hadn't been in the lion's den, but he had certainly been with the lion, seen its teeth, and had managed to come out alive with a pretty good deal. He was under no illusions his continued presence on this planet relied on making this work. Donald Munro was not a pleasant man.

There was still a lot more work to be done before the seller phoned back. Arranging a meeting place, finding onward buyers, the list went on. If this deal went ahead he wanted to move the stones on quickly. He had an uneasy feeling and he wanted them out of his sight as soon as possible.

With a last minute change of mind, Harry headed to his favourite cafe in Leather Lane. The thought of going to the office didn't appeal to him right now. Time to go and get a large mug of tea, a Tunnock's Teacake, and put the world to rights with the cafe owner.

An hour later, Harry had discussed the release of Nelson Mandela, the future of the Soviet Union, and the price of a decent pint. He decided to call it a day. No point in going back to his office now. Excellent. He would just be in time for rush hour, but first he had another phone call to make.

CHAPTER FIFTEEN
4th April 1990, Wapping, London

Donald came into his office like a battleship in full steam.

"Willie, get your arse in here," he called over his shoulder.

He dropped into the chair behind the desk as Willie came dashing through the door.

"Shut the door behind you."

Willie closed the double doors, raising his eyebrows at Lenny as he did so. He wasn't sure what the boss was all steamed up about but he was certain he was about to find out.

"What did you dig up on Harry Hart?"

Willie was Donald's most trusted man. He had been with him for the past twenty years. Donald relied on him not only for the word on the street, but to dispose of any 'inconveniences' Donald may have. Willie had connections everywhere, not only in the criminal world but in the police and judiciary. Many considered Willie to be a lovable rogue, which proved a book should not be judged by its cover.

"Not much, boss. He's as clean as they say. He's never done anything illegal as far as I can tell. No vices. Occasional girlfriend but no one steady. No one in his life right now. He's the average grey man in the street."

"So why the hell does he want to deal with me now?"

"He does?"

"Damn, sorry Willie. I haven't filled you in on the phone call and meeting."

Donald spent the next five minutes bringing Willie up to date with the day's proceedings.

"Well, if you ask me, boss, I'd say he knows full well the origin and he doesn't want anyone asking too many questions."

"You think?"

"Why else would he come to you? He can handle business on his own, but he has been known to share a deal with others."

"Ach you're probably right Willie. I'm being paranoid."

"Better safe than sorry, boss."

"Indeed, Willie, indeed. Which is why once this deal is over Mr Hart and I will be parting our ways, permanently, so to speak. I don't want to be sharing the deal and I don't want it biting my arse at a later date if you get my meaning."

"You thinking of him going for a cruise on the Thames boss?"

"Details, Willie. As long as Harry Hart will not be a future problem then I'll leave the details up to you."

CHAPTER SIXTEEN
5th April 1990, Aberdeen, Scotland

"You know, Steve, it really sucks."

"I have to agree."

"Agree to what? I haven't told you anything yet."

"You're not talking about your flying then?"

Andy laughed. "Cheeky bugger! No, you know I still enjoy it or I wouldn't be here right now would I? No, I mean being skint. Since the divorce, things have been going from bad to worse. I'm definitely going to lose the house now."

"Jeez, Andy. I'm really sorry, mate. I know you mentioned it might come to that, but I thought you'd manage to get it sorted."

"That's not the half of it. The rest of the creditors have got together and they're filing to have me made bankrupt."

"Oh, why didn't you tell me sooner? We might have been able to work something out. Isn't there any way you can stall for time or get the debt reduced? We could sort something."

"It's too late for that. I've been racking my brains, what little I have left of them, trying to think of a way to raise some more cash. I can sell the bike but that's about it, and that's not going to bring much."

"Now I know things are desperate if you're thinking of selling the monster. Are you sure there's nothing I can do? I don't have much, but if I can help in any way...?" Steve let the question hang.

"Thanks. I appreciate it, I really do, but short of robbing a bank there's not a lot can be done. Mind you, my bank manager reckons with my overdraft, I've already done that."

"Have you thought about it?" asked Steve quietly.

"What? Rob a bank?" He searched Steve's face. "Are you serious?"

"Hypothetically speaking of course."

"Not sure I would have the balls, and I certainly couldn't threaten anyone, so it would have to be a break in, not an armed robbery."

"So you don't fancy dressing up in a stocking, armed with a sawn-off chair leg. But in principle you wouldn't be bothered about stealing money?"

"It depends on who from. I don't want to mug any little old ladies, but in principle, I suppose not. Not that I would want anyone to suffer because of it, mind. I would never steal from an individual. Big companies are another matter. They take from us all the time. I probably wouldn't shed a tear over an insurance company having to foot the bill."

"So it has to be a business, with plenty of money, and definitely not a little old lady."

"Yeah that just about sums it up. Oh and there has to be no chance of getting caught."

"Right. A high value, zero risk heist, from a big company. I think if there was such a thing we might not be the only ones looking at it." Steve laughed at the thought.

"I didn't know we were looking at it."

"Neither did I, until now."

As they continued flying they both fell deep into their own thoughts. The only sound for the next few minutes was of the engines and rotor blades.

It was three in the morning and they were in the S-61N helicopter flight simulator at Aberdeen Airport. Housed in its own building, the simulator allowed pilots to practice procedures which would be unsafe on a real helicopter, and it saved expensive flying time. The simulator provided both a visual display and movement, making it a realistic experience. Both of them had jobs in the North Sea helicopter industry, but neither were pilots. Andy was a simulator engineer in Aberdeen. He was an incomer, a Sassenach, as many were who worked in the North Sea industry. Steve was a local, and worked as a helicopter engineer at Longside, near Peterhead.

In the long periods of sitting on a rock, fishing and waiting for something to happen, Steve had discovered Andy spent much of his spare time in the simulator when it wasn't being used by the aircrew. This usually meant in the early hours of the morning, but even then it was often busy. Andy invited him to come along and have a go at flying. Steve had jumped at the chance to have a play.

He watched as Andy flew the helicopter. He wasn't a natural pilot. Clumsy on the controls, he had to work hard to keep flying, especially when doing some of the more complex manoeuvres. No one was more surprised than Steve himself to find out he was a natural flyer. The helicopter became an extension of his own body. He made imperceptible inputs to the controls without even thinking about it.

When learning to drive a car, most learners have to think about every gear change, even looking down at the gear lever. Eventually, changing gear becomes second nature to the majority, but some remain clumsy throughout their lives. A rare few never have to go through that stage at all, almost as if born with the knowledge. And so it was with Steve and his flying.

"So what are we going to do about it?" he asked, breaking the silence.

"About what?"

"Jeez, Andy, are you a goldfish or what?"

"Oh, the money. I don't think there is anything that can be done. Here, you take over for a while. I'm tensing up."

Steve took over and immediately the helicopter settled down. He rolled the aircraft sharply to the right and began a tight spiral descent, levelling out a few feet off the ground.

"You are completely bonkers, you know that?" said Andy.

"Oh aye, as mad as they come, but you have to live a little."

"I'm glad this is a sim and not the real thing."

Steve said nothing for the next few minutes, concentrating on following the contours of the earth. He glanced across at Andy and pulled sharply back on the stick. Andy sat staring out of the windscreen, shaking like a leaf.

"Andy, you Okay?"

"What do you think?"

"I think we need to look at this logically. We, and please note I said we, will get this thing licked."

"Steve, you've got enough problems of your own, without worrying about me."

"What problems do I have, apart from having you as a mate? And as you are my mate, we will solve it."

Steve wasn't sure how yet, but whatever it was, it sure as hell wouldn't be legal.

CHAPTER SEVENTEEN
16th June 1990, Longside, Aberdeenshire

The airfield at Longside had few houses around it. Apart from the hangar door being locked there was no other security, and Steve had a copy of the key. Break in and steal a helicopter. What on earth had they been thinking when they came up with this idea? It sounded so simple when first put forward. The weekend was the only time they could do this. The helicopter was away from the base during the week, on a contract to the Northern Lighthouse Board. Unfortunately, weekends were also when people stayed up longer, walked home late from the pub, or a night out clubbing. Although night flights were rare from Longside, they were not unknown and Steve hoped anyone who heard him would not pay too much attention. There was nothing he could do about it even if someone did. He shrugged.

He knew his flight would be visible to any of the radars that covered the North Sea, both civilian and military. Although he couldn't be sure he would be tracked, he had no qualms about the radar operators following the first part of his flight.

For the second part he had to get underneath the radar, or at least be in the ground clutter on the display. Then the operators could not be sure of what they were seeing. RAF Buchan radar was not far down the road from Longside, and he knew how low the Buccaneers had to fly to get under the radar cover.

Since his discussion with Andy in the sim, Steve had amassed quite a collection of objects that would be expected to float if a helicopter crashed into the sea; seat cushions, maps and charts, spare life jackets. He had also prepared a 45-gallon drum that would sink and release its contents, a mixture of aviation fuel and waste oil. He had drilled a series of holes around the top of the drum, and then taped over them to prevent the fluid spilling out in flight. The tape ended in a big loop to be attached to a net under the helicopter.

Once the net opened, the tape would tear away under the weight of the falling drum. The other items he had collected would be with the drum in the net. He had carefully split the net down the middle and fastened the two halves together again with a pull cord. Weights attached to the sides of the net would make sure it sank when dropped into the sea. By deliberately flying at a higher altitude the inevitable search for the missing machine should be directed to the North Sea, as that would be the last radar trace of the helicopter and where the debris would be found.

Andy had dropped Steve at the south side of the airfield shortly before ten pm and headed straight back to the landing site. They had found a disused barn, a few miles off the Invermoriston to Kyle of Lochalsh road. The barn nestled in the hills; accessed by a bumpy track from the main road. The remote location and size made it the ideal choice. Here they would be safe from the prying eyes of any hill-walkers in the area during the day. The helicopter had to remain hidden for a few days.

Steve didn't fancy trying to get the helicopter inside by himself, but there were no guarantees Andy would make it back in time. It was hard enough with the two of them. They wouldn't have the luxury of the A-frame tow bar, it was simply too large to take with them. They would have to manhandle it inside instead.

He made his way to the middle of the disused part of the airfield and then settled down in the long grass to wait until midnight. As he lay there looking up at the stars, he set the alarm on his watch. Even though so many things were going through his mind, lying down here it would be too easy to fall asleep.

Steve loved the countryside, and this part of Scotland was blessed with more than its fair share of beauty. Here the land is pastoral; to the West the fields give way to the Grampian Mountains. A couple of miles to the East lies the North Sea and a salty tang in the air mixes with the scent of freshly cut grass; probably someone getting in their silage at this time of year. Miles of sand dunes stretch along the shoreline between Peterhead and Fraserburgh, and to the South a mixture of cliffs and sandy shores reach all the way to Aberdeen. It was a pity the climate wasn't a few degrees warmer. But then the area would undoubtedly be spoiled by weekend properties built by people with far more money than taste.

In the beam of the torch, the red paint seemed so much brighter. The Bolkow 105D sat in the centre of the hangar; tractor and ground-handling wheels still attached. He was relieved it was there. Although no flying had been planned for the aircraft when Steve had started his holidays, there had always been the outside chance of a last minute weekend charter.

It took over an hour for Steve to get things ready. He was lucky; the tractor had not been moved since bringing the aircraft inside. He jacked up the ground-handling wheels then lifted the tow bar, attaching it to the towing point on the front of the tractor. First he towed the helicopter to the fuel installation. He needed full tanks for the flight as it was almost on the limit of range for the Bolkow. They had already taken a 45-gallon drum of fuel up to the barn at the landing site, along with a hand pump to give them enough fuel for the job.

It wasn't completely dark; the summer nights in this part of the world never became pitch black. He felt exposed here. The apron area was visible from the road. Once he had squeezed as much as he could into the fuel tank he towed the helicopter to a revetment at the east end of the airfield. The banking built during WWII to protect aircraft from bomb blasts would also help to hide the sound of the helicopter when he started up.

The helicopter had two clam-shell doors at the back underneath the tail boom, which opened to reveal a cavernous load area which everyone called the boot. He removed the ground-handling wheels and put them in. The wheels would be needed at the landing site. He drove the tractor and tow bar back to the hangar, putting them back exactly where he had found them, minus one helicopter. He would love to see their faces in the morning.

The next task was to bring the drum and all the bits and pieces to put into the net. He had stashed the items in a shed, out on the airfield. He loaded up the forklift and headed back along the taxiway. As soon as he reached the revetment with the drum, Steve lowered it onto the concrete and switched off the fork lift engine. As the sound died away he heard a car coming along the road. A few moments later it swung into the car park next to the terminal building. The sign on the top announced 'Police.'

Steve froze. Marvellous, we haven't even started and we've been caught.

The headlights swung around and the car set off in the same direction as it had been heading. Steve breathed again, realising it was probably a routine patrol. Lucky they hadn't come a bit earlier when he was refuelling. He hoped they didn't come back this way too soon.

He crawled underneath the helicopter to attach the lifting strop onto the load hook. The other end of the strop connected to the weighted net which he laid out in front of the helicopter. This would not be an easy thing to deal with. The drum had to stand in front of the helicopter and would cause the net to swing when he lifted it off the ground. He had no experience of under slung loads apart from in the sim, and he would be a lot happier when he had dropped the load and released the net.

He passed the pull cord through the pilot's DV window. The window could be opened to allow the pilot to see out and ventilate the aircraft in the event of the cockpit filling with smoke. It was also handy for pilots to throw out cigarette ends when having an illicit smoke. He made a mental note to make sure the window was still open when he dropped the net. He didn't want a long length of cord whipping around the side of the helicopter. Once more he took the chance of being spotted by returning the forklift to the hangar, then jogged back to the revetment.

Steve climbed into the helicopter. This was his last chance to walk away. He settled himself into the seat pulling the straps of the harness over each shoulder before clipping them into the buckle. He pulled the harness tight. In the silence he imagined he could hear his heart beating. Maybe it wasn't his imagination. Maybe it really was that loud. He sat still for a few moments, composing himself, forcing his breathing to slow down. The sweat was running down the inside of his flight suit, making him uncomfortable. Perhaps he shouldn't have put it on until after all the donkey work had been done. Too late now. He looked around the cockpit. He was fond of the Bolkow. A workhorse of a helicopter. They were getting a little old now. This one smelled like an old machine. Oil, plastic, the countless numbers of bodies parking their backsides on these seats, all added to the aroma. All old aircraft had this smell, like old cars. To some it was as much a part of the enjoyment of working on these machines as anything else. You could keep your modern aircraft with their fancy computers. They had no character, no soul. This was a proper machine and flown by real pilots. He hoped he was up to the task of being a real pilot.

He did as much of his pre-flight checks as he could by torchlight; he wanted to retain as much power as he could in the aircraft battery for starting the engines. A battery cart would have meant getting out again to disconnect it after starting, and he didn't want to do that. To get in and out of the pilot seat on a running helicopter was a bad idea when you were on your own.

"Okay, battery master on, voltage good. Test the warning lights and the engine fire warning." The sound of the fire bell seemed incredibly loud in the darkness.

"Fuel on, power levers set, number two engine selected, press the button, number two turning, oil pressure, fuel flow, TGT rising, temperatures and pressures stabilised, start complete," Steve muttered out loud an abbreviated checklist. This was the easiest way for him to recall what he had memorised. He didn't want anyone to come across a handwritten checklist in the subsequent investigation into the theft. The full checklist had items in it he didn't need for this flight.

The Allison C250 was only a small engine but in the dead of night it sounded loud to Steve's ears. He was sure someone would hear it.

He repeated the same process for the number one engine.

"Okay all stable, all looking good, let's go."

Gradually he raised the collective lever until the helicopter went light on its skids.

He lifted the helicopter until he could move forward over the net, slowly increasing height until the load was clear of the ground.

He thought it best if he didn't hover taxi to the runway this time and elected instead to lift straight up, tilting the helicopter forward to gather speed, remembering he couldn't go too fast, or accelerate too quickly with his under-slung load.

Because of the wind direction he had to take off towards the West, but as soon as he was airborne he turned to the East and headed out toward the North Sea. On the way he passed over Peterhead town. With a bit of luck someone would remember hearing a helicopter flying out to sea. Once discovered missing, the police would be sure to make an appeal for information. On the other hand, helicopters flying out to sea were an everyday event here. He climbed steadily to 1500ft, knowing the military radar controllers would see him. They would be unlikely to be too concerned by traffic leaving Longside. Their job was to look for Russians coming in, not civilians going out. This would be unknown traffic, but heading away from their area, and their interest. The civilian radar at Aberdeen closed down at 11pm. They wouldn't be tracking him.

Thirty miles offshore Steve looked for ships in the area. The wake of a ship is quite visible at night, though not all boats were necessarily underway. There was a crescent moon over the horizon. Not a great deal of it but the silvery light dancing across the calm sea would help to highlight any wake. After a good look around, Steve couldn't see any vessels close enough to bother him so he descended in a slow spiral until he came into the hover fifty feet from the surface. He switched the transponder to standby and switched off the navigation lights and anti-collision beacon. The military radar controllers would have seen the loss of height, if they were paying attention to him, but he hoped they would assume it was a controlled descent to a ship. A tug on the release cord caused the helicopter to rise with the sudden reduction in weight. He knew the load had gone from the net.

He selected the hook release and dropped the net, hoping he had attached enough weights to make it sink. He wanted any search to concentrate on this area for a few days but if they found the net it might give the game away. It was better to take a chance dropping it here than to fly any distance with it flapping underneath the helicopter.

Keeping at fifty feet above the sea, Steve turned to fly north. He had to fly low level across an expanse of sea to avoid the military bases on the edge of the Moray Firth. He was less likely to be heard by staying out at sea. That was the easy part. Once over land he would fly into the mountains, low level, and in the dark.

"Doddle," he said to himself

CHAPTER EIGHTEEN
17th June 1990, Ceannacroc, Scottish Highlands

The Scottish Hydro Board Land Rover turned off the A87. The road led to a small hamlet on the Ceannacroc Estate. Hydro Board Land Rovers were not an uncommon site in this area. Nearby was Loch Cluanie. Along with Loch Loyne and a network of pipes they formed part of the Ceannacroc Hydro power station, which in turn formed part of the Great Glen Hydro Scheme. Water intakes higher up the valley supplied water to the scheme from the River Doe, and although the residents might have wondered why the Land Rover was heading up there in the middle of the night, they would not have thought it so out of the ordinary for it to warrant a call to the police. Andy saw no one as he drove slowly to keep down the noise on the single track road in the centre of the hamlet. He had made good time getting here after dropping off Steve, but he knew the helicopter would not be too far away by now. This was assuming he had managed to steal the helicopter in the first place, and had not flown into the sea or a hillside along the way. Steve had told him to wait for twenty-four hours and then get out again under the cover of darkness if he didn't make it.

The road had now become nothing more than a track following the course of the River Doe. Sheep pens dotted the countryside along the route as he climbed steadily into the hills. It was almost four miles later when Andy reached a fork in the track and swung the Land Rover to the left. Another two hundred yards and he could see the old barn in the growing daylight. Even though it was only 3am and sunrise was still almost an hour away, there was enough light to see without headlamps. It was one advantage of being in Northern Scotland a few days before the longest day. Unfortunately, he would also be visible to anyone else who might be around. People took walks at some strange times.

He parked the Land Rover inside the barn and switched on a small radio transmitter they had built. It transmitted a continuous carrier wave on the frequency of 339 KHz, the same as the non-directional beacon at Longside. These beacons, along with other types, were all over the country, allowing aircraft to navigate, even when they couldn't see the ground. The low power levels on both their own transmitter and the one at Longside, and the distance between them, meant there would be no possibility of them interfering with each other. Being on the same frequency had given Steve the chance to test the beacon at Longside without the worry of anyone accidentally picking up an unknown frequency.

The transmitter would be received on the helicopter's Automatic Direction Finding equipment, once Steve was close. They knew it wouldn't be all that accurate with all these hills around, and the range would be short, but something was better than nothing.

The main concern was Steve flying up the wrong valley somewhere along the route. All valleys looked similar in the half-light; sometimes even in the daytime it was hard to know which one you were in, but they had a plan to alleviate the problem.

The Bolkow was fitted with a Mk 15 Decca Navigator which showed the helicopter's position on a moving map display. A roll of special map paper mounted into a cassette, which slotted into the display head and scrolled up or down. A pointer moved side to side and could show the position of the helicopter as determined by the Decca receiver. They had spent some time marking the route on the Decca roll, and considerably longer poring over Ordnance Survey maps, to identify good landmarks. The Decca was there for confirmation to Steve he was still on the right route. Primary navigation was by Mk 1 eyeball, looking out of the window.

Andy cracked six glo-sticks and put four of them out on the corners of the flat area in front of the barn. The glo-sticks would hardly be needed by the time Steve arrived. The light would be pretty good by then, but at least it would help a little in marking out the area. He checked the wind direction and placed the remaining two outside the square to show the direction from where the wind was blowing. Steve would need to land into wind. He went back to the barn and settled down to wait.

When Andy first heard Steve's proposal he thought he was joking. When he realised he was serious he thought he was completely mad. What's more, he was doing it mainly for him. Sure, he would benefit from it too, but he only dreamt up the idea to get Andy out of a hole. It was typical of Steve that once he had made up his mind, he was going to throw himself into the project wholeheartedly. Every obstacle to achieving his goal was seen as a personal challenge, and he worked until it was overcome and the next one presented itself. This time he had excelled himself. Stealing a helicopter wasn't exactly an everyday event.

Andy asked himself once more why he had finally agreed to it. The truth was he believed totally in Steve and his abilities. Sure he made mistakes, but not when it really mattered. His mind was analytical, looking for all the possible outcomes in every stage of the planning. It was the old military adage of the seven Ps, piss poor planning produces piss poor performance, and Steve's planning was relentless. The biggest potential flaw in this plan was Steve not being a pilot, and although he had spent considerable time in the sim, he had relatively little time flying for real, and none flying alone in the dark at low level over the sea and in the mountains.

He looked at his watch. Three forty-five. Steve should have been here fifteen minutes ago. They had allowed for fifteen minutes either way, but now they were heading for overtime, and still no sign of the helicopter. He should hear it well before it got there, but all Andy could hear was the gently stirring breeze, the occasional call of an owl and the barking of a fox. He hoped nothing had gone wrong.

CHAPTER NINETEEN
17th June 1990, Scottish Highlands

The fir tree brushed the underside of the helicopter. Steve swore and lifted the collective lever, only a fraction, but enough to lift the helicopter clear of the trees. Damn these night vision goggles.

He needed to relax; to sense the helicopter. Not an easy task when flying low level, especially as his previous experience was entirely in the simulator. His tight grip on the controls made his flying twitchy. The trees flashed by incredibly close, his speed accentuated by their proximity. He must get a hold of himself. There would be no second chances here. A mistake now would be his last.

He had been awake for twenty-two hours and pumping adrenalin for most of them. From the start he had known it would be hard to keep his concentration. Inevitably his mind would wander, making certain they had everything covered. The fatigue didn't help, but the nature of the task made that unavoidable. A timescale outside his control had led to a high risk plan; one which he now considered would probably kill him.

After the brush with the tree, he thought it prudent to fly a little higher, being clear of the military bases and the major towns now. He lifted up the night vision goggles and found he could see clearly. Unless he flew into a deep valley, still in shadow, he no longer needed them. It proved to be a stroke of luck removing them. He scanned the sky around the helicopter and spotted the lights of another aircraft in the distance, over to his left. Silhouetted against the dawn sky he recognised it as a Sea King. Probably a search and rescue flight out of Lossiemouth. They were on a converging course. His own helicopter was not displaying any lights. He would be lost in the dark backdrop of the mountains to them.

He couldn't continue on this course or they would spot him. There wasn't enough fuel to hover until they had passed, and that would expose him to anyone on the ground who was up at this time. Helicopters were not unusual in this part of the world, but one hovering in the early morning would attract attention. Nor did he have enough fuel to reverse his course for a few minutes. Turning left would bring him closer to the helicopter, turning right too close to the mountains.

The only sensible course of action was to land. He would have to land on an unknown site, in the semi-light and amongst the trees, a risky proposition. Deep shadows formed in the Scottish forest below. The nearest fields were under the flight path of the other machine. Once more in this operation his choices had become limited. He pulled the goggles back down and searched the deep shadows below for a suitable place to land. So much for the plan Steve, so much for the plan.

CHAPTER TWENTY

17th June 1990, Scottish Highlands

Steve looked around for a suitable area to land and saw a forest road with a wide clearing to one side of it. It was probably where logs were stacked before the trucks took them away. Logging was widespread in Scotland. Steve didn't like the immediate aftermath of logging operations. Large tracts of bare land turning grey as the stumps and abandoned logs started to weather. Occasional trees standing upright with most of the branches stripped bare, not worth felling, the sole survivors of an arboreal Armageddon.

Commercial vandalism is how Steve thought of it.

It didn't take the land long to recover, a few years at the most, but it still looked awful in the meantime.

Steve headed for the open area. The clearing wasn't as light as he would like, and there was always the chance of hitting an unseen cable or a branch. That would ruin the day. He set the helicopter down as gently as he could. The ground was rutted but dry, the long skids of the Bolkow resting across the top of them. He was going to have to shut down and give time for the other helicopter to move out of the area. He thought it best to stay on the ground for around fifteen minutes; long enough to let the Sea King get out of the area and short enough not to be discovered.

After the rotor blades had come to a stop, he got out to stretch his legs and answer the call of nature. Like a lot of pine forests it was eerily silent, the only sound being from the helicopter, the ticking of the cooling metal like miniature gunshots in the stillness of the forest.

Any other time he would have enjoyed the silence but with his nerves on edge, every sound made him jump. After what seemed to be hours, yet was only the fifteen minutes he timed, he got back in and went through the start-up checks again. Ideally he should have let the engines cool down a bit more before starting, but he didn't have time.

He lifted straight up out of the clearing; turning the helicopter through three hundred and sixty degrees, he had a good look around making sure there were no more surprises in store for him, then set course again for the landing site.

Andy must be panicking by now Steve thought, but there wasn't a lot he could do about it at the moment.

It was light now and he was glad of the time spent looking at maps and picking out features to help him navigate. He knew he was on the right course as landmark after landmark popped into view. He was beginning to enjoy himself which came as a surprise, considering all of the possible outcomes of this little escapade.

He realised this was the last valley before the landing site. This part was almost over and soon they would be moving on to phase two. It wasn't going to get any easier but as far as

Steve was concerned this had been the riskiest. They could still get caught, but now he was less likely to die as the rest of the flying was going to be in daylight and in full view of the public.

The helicopter crested the next ridge and there they were, six dots of green light marking out the landing area.

Having made it this far he thought it would be ironic if he made a balls up of the landing.

He set the Bolkow down in the middle of the marked area and shut down.

As soon as the rotors stopped, Andy yanked open the door.

"Where the hell have you been?" he shouted at Steve.

"Good to see you too, mate," Steve said, laughing. "I had a spot of bother with the RAF and had to land for a little while."

Steve filled him in with the details of the flight as they retrieved the glo-sticks, before manhandling the helicopter into the barn. They couldn't waste any time in getting it under cover. This was hillwalking country and some people enjoyed ridiculously early starts.

Steve had a thought. "The Sea King didn't come over this way did it?"

"I didn't hear it. If I had, I would have assumed it was you. Why?"

"Cos we had some nice bright glo-sticks out is why. We didn't think that one through did we? We should have done it when you heard me."

"Too late now. If they saw them, well they saw them, but I doubt it. I didn't hear anything until you came, so they couldn't have come this way. In any case if I had put them out when I heard a helicopter, I would have done it for them, so they still would have seen them. Remember I work the sim. I don't have the ear for different helicopter sounds that you have."

"Yeah, true. I keep forgetting you're just an amateur..." Steve ducked just in time to avoid getting clipped across the top of the head. "Now, now. Best you don't wound your pilot."

"I'll give you wounding, you cheeky sod."

"Let's get the daily inspection done and then back to camp to get some kip," said Steve. "Our body clocks are going to be all over the place."

Steve had a good look around the helicopter, making sure nothing was loose or broken and checking the oil levels in the engines and gearboxes.

"Do a trip," he said closing the engine cowling.

He turned to Andy and showed him the piece of tree he had found wedged in the cross tube of the skids.

"Erm...this is a piece of the tree I hit."

"You hit a tree?" Andy exclaimed. "What the hell were you doing so low?"

"It's those bloody night vision goggles. They flatten everything. No sense of distance when you're wearing them. It's like looking down a green tunnel. The tree looked a lot further away than it was."

"Bloody hell, Steve you could have been killed."

"I didn't know you cared."

"I don't, but my car keys are locked in your house."

"Heartless bugger."

Before bringing out the Land Rover, they had a good look around with binoculars. Once they were as sure as they could be no one would see them, they quickly brought it out and shut the barn door again.

They headed back down the track that Andy had driven up earlier, but they weren't going back through the village. Three miles from the barn, they turned left and crossed over the river on a narrow bridge. In another two miles they arrived at a smaller track that led into the adjacent forest. It was really no more than two ruts that had been worn into the forest floor and was now getting overgrown. Once they were out of sight of the main track they stopped. This was going to be home for the next three nights.

CHAPTER TWENTY-ONE
17th June 1990, Aberdeen, Scotland

Nicky hated Sundays. Nothing ever happened on Sundays as far as he was concerned, especially in this part of the world. In fact nothing happened on any day here. Nicky believed his destiny was to be in the bustling newsroom of a major national newspaper. Instead, he was stuck in this grey, miserable excuse for a city that was Aberdeen, working for the local rag, the Press and Journal, or P & J as it was known to the locals. Perhaps the fact Nicky believed the city was always grey and miserable owed more to his mind-set than to reality. It might not be on the French Riviera, but it was not as bleak as many made out, and certainly not as wet. It was grey though. It was known as the Granite City for a reason.

Nicky's biggest problem was he simply wanted to be elsewhere. Admittedly, the offices themselves were hardly conducive to a bright and breezy disposition. The open plan layout was more suited to parking cars, than a place for working people. Every desk had the clutter of a teenager's bedroom, often spilling over onto its neighbour; occasionally onto the floor. The desks huddled together in little congregations, each with their own part to play in the delivery of a vital breakfast ingredient for many, the News.

Nicky grew up in the East End of London, where the scars of the Second World War were still evident and part of Nicky's childhood. In the swinging sixties and the super seventies, what East End kid hadn't played on a bomb site? Prefab homes were still a common sight. Intended to be a stop-gap measure for the housing shortage, they lasted longer than the war itself. His childhood had been tough although he hadn't realised it at the time. As far as he knew that was the way life was. His father had been a docker in the East London docks. Docklands in the sixties and seventies was a continuous series of strikes and Nicky's father spent as much time at home as he did at work. He knocked back the pints in the local pub when not working. That was when Nicky made himself scarce, rather than suffer the beatings that would inevitably follow.

On strike days, after school, Nicky spent his time equally playing with his mates down at the river, or when he could get away unseen, in the local lending library. At first the librarians were wary of this scruffy East End kid wanting to spend time with their precious books, but they came to realise he had a genuine interest in reading, and allowed him access not only to the more adult books, but also to the prized reference section. An avid reader, Nicky learned there was more to life than leaving school as soon as possible and either thieving or getting a job in the docks, or as some did, combining the two. Unlike many of the kids he grew up with, Nicky didn't descend into a life of crime. He had a head on his shoulders and he wanted to be somebody. He wanted to be Prime Minister. All the other kids laughed at him when he told them of his ambitions.

"I'm going to be somebody one day, you see if I don't."

They still laughed, even when he got offered a place and a scholarship to study politics at Glasgow University. Despite the brutal relationship with his father, he knew he would have been proud. A pity he had not lived to see it. The years of heavy work and even heavier drinking had finally taken its toll, and he had passed away at the age of fifty-three.

At university, Nicky found he didn't like politics. The subject bored him to tears, and he soon realised his desire to be the Prime Minister was born from a wish to be recognised, rather than any burning ambition to enter the political arena. With continued determination, he remained conscientious in his studies and consistently achieved high marks.

A small advertisement on the notice board one day attracted his attention. The Glasgow University Guardian, the student-run newspaper, was looking for volunteer reporters. Ever since its inception in 1932 the newspaper had broken stories that some of the nationals had later taken. It numbered several high-profile politicians and journalists amongst its alumni.

On a whim Nicky decided to give it a go, and set about writing an article he knew something about, drink and violence. He was delighted when the paper accepted and published it. It was a thrill to see his name in print at the top of the page, and he wanted more.

Several articles followed, but the ones that gave him the most pleasure were those that exposed something about a company or individual they did not want the public to know about, such as a lecturer paying regular visits to the ladies offering their services in Blytheswood Square, or the agency letting out student accommodation that should have been condemned.

To uncover the grubby secret lives of other people was something he not only enjoyed, but to his surprise, something he was very good at.

After graduating with an honours degree in politics, he set out to find a job in journalism. Unfortunately, so did numerous others, many of whom had far greater journalistic experience than reporting for a student newspaper.

Nicky's dream of being the next top investigative journalist fell by the wayside, along with his aspirations of being the next Prime Minister, and he accepted a lowly-paid job with the P & J. It hadn't dampened his enthusiasm for digging up the dirt. But the dirt around here didn't have the same attraction to him as the dirt around London, and he couldn't wait to get a break with one of the Nationals in Fleet Street. He knew it would only be a matter of time before the right story would fall in his lap, and goodbye Aberdeen.

Nicky sat staring into space at his desk in the newsroom, toying with a pen and only half paying attention to the police band scanner sat on his desk. The usual reports of burglaries, vandalism and domestic abuse littered the airwaves, and he was never going to make a name for himself covering this sort of dross. He needed something juicy to get his teeth into.

A piece on the latest carnival queen to be crowned was sitting in front of him. Not the pinnacle of investigative journalism he had hoped for.

"Stolen helicopter," seeped into his consciousness, snapping him back to reality. Did they really just say that? He listened carefully to the one-sided message.

Unfortunately, the way the Police radios worked he was only able to hear half of the conversation. The other half was on a different frequency. He gleaned enough from this monologue to know a helicopter had gone missing from Longside Airfield.

He had no idea who Control was speaking to, but he had to assume it was CID, and not the ordinary plod.

Nicky grabbed the scanner, his jacket from the back of the chair and his bag from the side of the desk. He startled several others in the room as he dashed towards the door, shouting over his shoulder to the editor that he needed to get to Longside for a breaking story. The editor opened his mouth to speak, then slowly closed it as he realised he would be talking to a swinging door.

CHAPTER TWENTY-TWO
17th June 1990, Logierieve, Aberdeenshire

DCI MacIntyre was in the conservatory overlooking his garden and eating breakfast, whilst still in his dressing gown. The house was the former railway station at Logierieve, a stone's throw south of Ellon. Once part of the Great North of Scotland Railway, the line was closed to passengers as part of the Beeching cuts and altogether several years later. The original platforms were still in place, but the track itself had long since gone.

Mac's house was the eastbound part of the station and had an extensive garden backing onto Logierieve Woods. Apart from the occasional car passing on the adjacent B-road, it was a quiet place, any traffic sound deadened by the bushes and trees surrounding the property. The garden itself was lower than the road which rose up on an embankment to cross over the railway bridge. Such a large garden needed a lot of tending, which Mac had loved to do with his wife Helen, right up until she was taken from him four years earlier. She had been travelling back from Aberdeen late one evening, when her car had left the road, overturning several times before coming to rest in a field. Knowing Mac personally, the crash investigators had worked extremely hard on the case, but had been unable to explain why the accident had happened. Mac had been devastated, and even though time is supposed to be a great healer, he found it hung heavily on his hands.

He spent a lot more time at work now, but Sunday morning was pretty much sacrosanct. Sundays were for making a full Scottish breakfast, to be slowly consumed whilst reading the Sunday papers. He was grumbling at a story in *Scotland on Sunday* when the phone rang in the lounge. Tempted to ignore it, he knew it had to be important if someone risked disturbing him on a Sunday.

"MacIntyre," he announced into the handset.

"Grant here, Sir," the voice said at the other end.

"Grant, you do realise it is 11am on a Sunday morning don't you? Has a war started?"

"Morning, Sir. No, Sir. Ah...no one is dead, but we do have a missing helicopter...Sir."

"Missing as in crashed?"

"No, Sir, missing as in not where it should be. Staff at Bond Helicopters have reported they have a helicopter missing at Longside. Well, it's not at Longside. That's the point. It appears to be stolen. It was there last night, and this morning it isn't."

"How on earth do you steal a helicopter? You can't exactly put it in your pocket and walk out with it. Are they sure it isn't out somewhere?"

"Certain, Sir. It was due to go out tomorrow morning."

Mac let out a sigh. It looked as if he wasn't going to have his relaxing Sunday.

"Where are you now?"

"Peterhead nick. I came here as soon as I heard, wanted to check on the details first before calling you."

"Okay," Mac sighed, "I'll meet you there. I'll get a team together from here and get them up to Peterhead."

Mac hung up. He paused for a few moments to gather his thoughts. He was getting too old for this. Thank goodness his retirement was close at hand. He wasn't going to be wealthy, but with his pension he would be comfortable.

He stepped into the shower. The hot water ran off his taut muscles. He liked to keep himself in shape. His only concession was the weekly fry up and an occasional buttery, a croissant-like piece of bread peculiar to the North East of Scotland; delicious, but as its name implied, oozing with butter. Just because he was getting old, it did not mean he had to be unhealthy: Mac had no intention of letting himself go; it would have been so easy to do so after Helen's death.

An hour later, Mac swung his Range Rover into the car park at Longside Airfield. DS Grant came across to meet him.

"You look like a seventies American detective in those sunglasses," Mac grumbled.

The day was turning into a beauty with not a cloud in the sky.

"Thank you, Sir."

"It wasn't a compliment."

The relationship between the two was generally good. Mac thought Grant was going to make an excellent DI and had a good future ahead of him as long as he listened and learnt how to do it the proper way, Mac's way. Grant had been the one to break the news to Mac about Helen's death, the worst moment of his life.

"Okay Alan, fill me in with the basics. We'll do a full brief back at the nick with the team," said Mac.

"The early shift arrived at 0700 and, as per usual at the weekend, had a cuppa before going to unlock the hangar."

"Where was that?"

"There's a canteen at the other end of the terminal building. They unlock the far end and get the keys to the hangar from there."

"Any sign of forced entry?"

"Apparently not, Sir. Local Uniform had a quick nose around when they got here. About 0730 they unlocked the hangar and found the helicopter was missing. It had arrived Friday afternoon and was due to go out Monday morning."

"Who has keys to the building?"

"Quite a lot of people apparently. We've got the Chief Engineer on his way. The Operations Director is on his way from Aberdeen too."

Mac stared into the distance; this was a new one to him. He had known a lot of things stolen in his time, but a helicopter was a first.

"Forensics?"

"Not looking likely, Sir. Lots of prints from lots of people, what you would expect really."

Mac grunted. This would not be an easy one by the looks of it.

"Right. Leave one of your boys here, and a couple of Uniforms. They can have a chat with the Chief Engineer and Operations Director when they get here. We'll get back to the nick and see where we go from here."

"DCI MacIntyre."

Mac turned around to find the source of the voice. Nicky bloody Rolands.

He turned back to Grant.

"Bollocks. How did he find out?"

"I dunno, Sir. He was here when I arrived, tramping around asking questions of the uniforms. I told him if he set foot out of the car park again I would nick him for interfering with a police investigation."

"You are getting more like me every day, and that is a compliment."

"Thank you... I think, Sir."

Mac wasn't like other officers when it came to the press. He didn't think of them as the enemy, or a useful ally. He thought of them as the devil incarnate. On one of his cases as a young DI, the press had leaked details allowing a killer to avoid a trap they had set for him. Several days later he struck again. After that, Mac had slightly less than no time for the press.

"Rolands. As it seems you were here before we were, I can only come to two possible conclusions. Either you were involved, or you have been listening to a scanner."

"It's not illegal to own a scanner," said Nicky sullenly. "Anyway, involved in what, Mac?"

"Firstly it's 'DCI Macintyre' to you, though 'Sir' will suffice. Secondly, owning the scanner may not be illegal but listening to a broadcast, for which you don't have the authority to listen to, is. So unless you want me to nick you for offences under the Wireless and Telegraphy Act 1949, I suggest you scarper smartish."

"Give me a break, DCI MacIntyre; I'm only looking for a story."

"You can have one from the press release if and when we make one."

"But..."

"Are you still here?" growled Mac.

Mac watched Nicky walk back to his car.

"Right, Grant. We'll use your car and pick up mine from here later. Back to the nick via the village. It's your turn for the butteries."

"It's always my turn," muttered Grant.

"What was that?"

"I said it would be my pleasure, Sir."

"That's what I thought."

Mac turned his head to the side window whilst putting on his seatbelt. He couldn't help a little smile.

CHAPTER TWENTY-THREE
17th June 1990, Peterhead, Aberdeenshire

"Okay, a wee bit of hush please, lads. DS Grant is going to fill us in," announced Mac to the assembled group of men.

DS Alan Grant looked across to Mac who motioned for him to carry on. This was his patch, and although DI Kerr was going to be in charge of day to day running with Mac in overall command, Grant had been involved from the start. Mac was more than happy for him to bring everyone up to date.

The normal complement of four Detective Constables and one Detective Sergeant had been supplemented by three more DC's, and a DI. The surprise to one or two in the room was the presence of Mac. All the officers knew each other, and most had worked together at some point. Clearly something serious was afoot if Mac was there in person, especially on a Sunday.

The briefing room of Peterhead police station, a rambling old Victorian building in the centre of the town was feeling cramped with so many officers present.

Grant started to speak.

"Okay, some of you ken what this is about, but some don't, so I'll start at the beginning. At some time between 1700 hours last night and 0700 hours this morning a helicopter was stolen from Bond Helicopters hangar at Longside."

A couple of the officers exchanged puzzled glances.

"The helicopter is a Bolkow Bo105D, registration Golf Bravo Delta Yankee Zulu. It's currently on contract to the Northern Lighthouse Board and was due out tomorrow morning. There was no sign of forced entry at the premises. I think it would be safe to assume the helicopter was flown out as enquiries indicate it would take a fair bit of preparation to transport by road, not to mention the fact it would be easy to spot on the back of a truck, even by Uniform."

Grant's pointed dig brought a few chuckles, but had any of the uniformed officers heard it, they would have known it to be banter. Uniform and CID often socialised together at the smaller police stations. Serious friction was nipped in the bud before it got out of hand. Ironically, they were busy doing some of the legwork for the detectives in the room; out gathering statements and seeking witnesses.

Grant continued. "The theoretical range is somewhere in the region of 300 miles. Uniform are carrying out door to door enquiries at the properties surrounding the airfield. National Air Traffic Services at Aberdeen have been contacted. Unfortunately their hours of operation are 0600 to 2300 so no radar service was operating during the night when it is suspected the helicopter was taken. They're keeping an eye out now for any unknown traffic in range of their radar. We have also contacted the MOD to see if the radar station at Buchan spotted anything. The official line at the moment is they can neither confirm nor deny if they did or did not see anything. No surprise there then. Enquiries are continuing in that direction."

That brought a few murmurs around the room. The MOD was not known for their immediate co-operation to any enquiries.

"As I've said, there was no sign of forced entry and the hangar was still locked, so it would appear the perpetrators had a key. At this stage we are assuming more than one person was involved. The fact they appear to have had a key makes it more than likely someone on the inside is involved. We have asked Bond for a list of employees who would have access, and a list of pilots. Forensic examination has turned up a multitude of prints, as would be expected at a workplace, but so far we have nothing else."

Grant scanned the room then looked at Mac. "That's as far as it goes for now, Sir."

Mac had been perched on the edge of a desk whilst DS Grant gave his briefing. He stood to address the assembled officers.

"Well, gentlemen. You don't need me to tell you the implications of this are very serious. It has been declared a major incident and has gone to the top straight away, and I don't only mean our top. The PM has asked to be kept up to date. Special Branch are also going to be all over it, and no doubt a few of the boys in trench coats will make an appearance."

There were a few groans in the room.

"Aye right, pipe down. I know how much you love our colleagues but we have to consider the theft might be related to our friends over the water in Ireland. The Royal Residences at Balmoral, Holyrood and Castle of May immediately spring to mind as possible targets. Oil and gas installations are also vulnerable, production platforms, St. Fergus or the Forties oil pipeline at Cruden Bay. I know, apart from the one incident at Sullom Voe, there have been no attacks in Scotland, but that doesn't mean there won't be."

Several pipelines from the North Sea oil fields came ashore at the gas processing plant at St. Fergus, which was a sprawling complex a few miles north of Peterhead. A number of oil companies had processing plants in the complex to clean the gas and deliver it to the adjacent British Gas plant for distribution throughout the UK. Hitting this complex would put a serious dent in the UK gas production. The oil pipeline from the Forties field came ashore a couple of miles south of Cruden Bay, to a pumping station. This station also received liquid products by pipeline from St. Fergus. An attack from the air on either of these would be difficult to stop, and could have a substantial, even devastating, effect on the economy.

"DI Kerr is going to be running this and I will be overseeing. Until we can either recover the helicopter or arrest those involved — or in an ideal world, both — we are going to be balls out on this one. DS Grant has filled you in on what we know so far. Now I'll hand you over to DI Kerr."

DI Graham Kerr stood up.

"Right. We don't have much to go on other than a helicopter is missing. The theft could be purely that. I don't know if there is a market in stolen aircraft but I would imagine they would be difficult to pass on. It could be the IRA are looking to do something spectacular, or it's going to be used for some other purpose. Anyone got any thoughts?"

Grant asked "What about the prison?"

Built in the late nineteenth century, Peterhead prison was a forbidding granite building on the headland to the south of Peterhead Harbour. It housed some of the most dangerous and disruptive prisoners in Scotland. It was a place many would love to leave early.

"Good point. Get onto Governor Coyle and put him in the picture."

"We have no idea which way they headed then?" asked DC Iain Alexander.

"No, they could have gone anywhere. Without any radar information, we really don't know."

"Glad we've narrowed it down then. Needle and haystack spring to mind."

"Aye. It gives us a search area covering the whole of Scotland, North of England and as far as the coast of Norway, but unless we get indications to the contrary we will assume Norway and England are not the destination. The Deputy Chief Constable is giving a press conference later, in time to get this on the evening news and into tomorrow's papers. We are going to need public help with this one."

There was a knock at the door and a uniformed officer popped his head round. "Sorry to bother you but this has just come in, thought you might like to see it straight away, Sarge." He handed DS Grant a piece of paper.

Grant quickly scanned it.

"A supply ship on its way back from the Forties has reported spotting some oil and debris in the water about thirty miles east of here, they fished a bit out. Seems it was an aircraft life jacket with 'Bond Helicopters' stencilled on it."

"Let's not jump to conclusions," said Mac, "but it would be a relief if we do find the helicopter there. In the meantime let's assume there is another explanation. As soon as we finish here I'll follow this up and see if we need to get a search vessel on the go."

Kerr continued, "On the plus side, helicopters are hard to move quietly, so we may get lucky and get a lead from the public. The minus is every helicopter that moves over the next few days will be reported to us. At the moment we want to hear from anyone who heard a helicopter Saturday night or early Sunday morning."

"Any high value arty farty stuff going on in the area? You know, exhibitions of paintings, sculptures that sort of thing." This was from DC Forbes.

"It's a thought, Brian. You run with that for the time being. See what you can get from the Tourist Board, they should know what's going on. Whilst you're on it, you might want to give the castles and stately homes a warning they might be targets," said Kerr.

"Anything else?"

A few shakes of the head and a couple of officers mumbled, "No Sir."

"Okay. Colin, Willie, Robbie and Angus, you start following up with the staff. We will need prints from everyone and their whereabouts last night. Uniform will be giving you a hand once the door to door enquiries are finished. Alan once you are wrapped up with the Governor, I want you get back on to the MOD to see if they have anything and keep on at them until they give a straight answer. Also get back on to NATS and see if a national radar might have been able to see them. We need an idea of where they were headed. Iain, I want you to talk to the Bond senior staff. See if they have recently sacked anyone, or if there's someone with a grievance. Has anyone been acting oddly recently? Jimmy, you follow up on anything Uniform comes up with on the door to door. Everyone clear? Good. Let's get to it then."

CHAPTER TWENTY-FOUR
18th June 1990, Kyle of Lochalsh, Scottish Highlands

Roddy put the cover back on the panel after carefully tucking in the wires so they would look like any of the others in the exchange. He didn't want anyone else to stumble across these. He would have liked to have done this a little closer to the time, closer to when it was needed, but he had so much to do. The chance of it being discovered was slim unless someone had to fault-find the line. He wasn't the only BT engineer in the area. He would try to make sure any fault-finding on these circuits was done by himself but he couldn't guarantee it.

He had made a similar alteration at the exchange in Invermoriston. Now he could connect himself anywhere on the phone network and take control of the phone lines to the Cluanie Inn and the call box outside, as well as the Kyle of Lochalsh police station. Even shutting them down if he wanted.

His next task would be the difficult one. He had to place a unit in the cable leading from the police radio transceiver to the antenna, at Kyle police station. He had no idea what it was for. He had only been told how to connect it. He didn't care. They were paying him enough to not ask questions.

As a BT engineer he had access to the police telephone system in the station and he could come and go pretty much as he pleased. He was supposed to sign in and out, but as it was such a small community no one ever enforced the rules, unless the brass were visiting from Inverness. Placing the box in the station was too risky. If discovered it wouldn't take a genius to work out who had put it there.

The plan was to put the box on the roof. That way he only had to break into the antenna feeder cable. Having a built-in battery pack made the box bulky. It would be visible. Roddy was relying on no one paying attention to the antenna. The exterior of the building and antenna mast were both white. The white box would appear to be part of the original installation. Unless someone from the police Comms Department paid a visit, he doubted anyone would notice it at all.

Of course, he still had to climb on the roof of a police station, in a residential area and probably with at least one officer inside. The rural station did not have a constant stream of officers in and out of the building, making the task slightly easier but the antenna was in full view of anyone passing. He would wait until the early hours of the morning before his attempt to fit the unit. Even then he would be taking a chance. He figured the best way was to go around the back of the building and clamber up on the roof out of sight. He would be exposed for about ten minutes at the most, connecting the box. Whoever had made it had done a good job. All he had to do was cut the antenna co-axial cable, strip it back and screw it into the terminal block inside. No messing around with connectors. Quick and simple, just the way he liked it.

Roddy looked at the time. There were still several hours to kill, so he killed them the best way he knew. He set the alarm on his watch, climbed into the front of his transit van and got his head down. He was never one to waste time doing something when he could be sleeping.

CHAPTER TWENTY-FIVE
18th June 1990, North Sea

"There doesn't appear to be anything down there, Chief Inspector," said the captain of the Royal Navy survey ship, HMS Herald.

"I know some fishermen would agree with you there," said Mac. "How certain are you?"

"I would say ninety percent unless we're in the wrong place of course. We took into account the time you believe the crash occurred, if there was one, and the time when the debris was found. We worked out the drift and calculated the probable area for the crash site. There's still a margin for error, but I'm sure we covered most of the area. I understand the aircraft has two underwater locator beacons, one on the flight recorder and one on the fuselage. We've heard nothing. I would also have expected more debris. It's a pity we didn't get a positive position from a radar plot."

"Yeah. Shame the RAF lost interest in the flight as soon as they saw it was going offshore. Mind you we had to push to get that much information."

"That's the RAF for you, can't keep them interested in anything except the next leave chit. You must have friends in high places, Chief Inspector. You managed to get us diverted."

"I think you can thank a certain Iron Lady for that. As you can imagine there is a wee bit of a panic going on with so many Royal residences around here. Not to mention all the oil installations. Until we either know where it is, or who has it, we're all getting our arses kicked from above."

The Commander laughed. "Nice to know there's a rank structure in Civvy Street too."

"Aye, the only upside is I get to kick arses too. Takes some of the pain away."

Sometimes Mac wondered why he had chosen a career in the police. He had always loved the sea and at one time had toyed with the idea of a career in the merchant navy. Travelling the world and getting paid for it appealed to him. When he met Helen the thought of being away from her for months at a time was no longer quite so appealing. Right now, on the bridge of HMS Herald he was enjoying himself. He would have preferred a rougher sea, but then again the job would probably have been impossible if it had been.

He looked out of the large windows and wished he had more money put away for his retirement. Perhaps then he would have bought himself a decent-sized yacht and set off on a cruise without end. That wasn't to be. Even with the insurance pay out from Helen's death, he couldn't afford to do that.

The MOD had been asked if they could supply a ship to search the suspected crash site, so it was an unexpected piece of luck that HMS Herald was on its way back from the Rosyth Naval Base, to continue with an oceanographic survey in the Norwegian Sea. They had agreed to divert the Herald into

Aberdeen so that Mac could board her for the search. That was yesterday, and since then she had been following a search pattern, looking for anomalies on the sea bed that would indicate something was down there that shouldn't be.

Mac had spent a good night aboard as a guest of the Wardroom. He felt like a distinguished visitor indeed. He could not fault the Navy on their hospitality. In some ways it was a shame to leave the ship. Unfortunately, with the news it was unlikely the helicopter had crashed, they would need to concentrate on searching in the haystack again.

"Well, I suppose that wraps it up then. What time do you expect to get back into harbour?"

"We aren't going back, Chief Inspector."

"I've no intention of swimming so how am I supposed to get ashore?"

The Commander smiled. "Your chariot will be here in twenty minutes. You're about to get a taste of inter-service co-operation."

Mac looked puzzled.

"There's an RAF Sea King on its way to collect you and drop you off at Aberdeen Airport."

"Ah," said Mac, "I didn't think your deck would be big enough for one of them."

"It's not," said the Commander.

"Then how on earth...oh!" said Mac, as the realisation hit him, "you don't mean..?"

"Yes, I do," said the Commander with a grin. "You're going to be winched off, which is why you're now going to go below and get yourself into a survival suit."

A rating was waiting nearby, ready to take Mac below.

"Oh goody." Mac's tone made it clear he didn't feel so good about it at all.

"Now you get the idea of why we like our boats," said the Commander. "If this one goes wrong, we all get into smaller ones. If that yellow-painted collection of bolts and rivets flying in close formation goes wrong, you're relying on a waterproof suit to keep you alive, and they don't work too well as parachutes."

"They have life rafts don't they?" Mac paused. "Why am I even having this conversation?"

The Commander laughed. "Sorry, I couldn't help it. Anyway we can always come and rescue you if anything does go wrong."

"Much obliged," Mac replied. He smiled at the Commander. "Thanks for your hospitality. I've really enjoyed myself."

"Our pleasure," replied the Commander as they shook hands.

"This way, Sir." The rating escorted Mac off the bridge.

They worked their way aft to the hangar. Herald had originally been equipped with a Westland Wasp helicopter, but the hangar was now empty. Mac was shown how to put on the suit and given some disposable ear plugs to put in.

"You're going to need those, Sir," said the rating. "Once the winch-man gets on deck, follow his instructions and you'll be fine."

Mac nodded his acknowledgement.

The Sea King approached the stern of the ship, gradually matching the forward speed of the vessel, and twenty feet above the deck. The winch-man sat in the doorway of the helicopter; as soon as it was in position over the deck he was winched down. He unhooked himself from the winch cable and signalled the winch operator. The helicopter moved away from the ship and flew round in a large circle to approach the ship again. In the meantime the winch-man briefed Mac on what he had to do — which was basically nothing. It was to be a double lift with Mac and the RAF crewman going up at the same time. By the time Mac was in the strop, the helicopter was back over the deck and lowering the hook. The winch-man connected the hook onto the strop and signalled for them to be lifted.

Mac was aware of rising quickly off the deck and a strong draft. He was also aware of the world spinning around. Spinning on the cable was a common occurrence once in the down draft of the helicopter. Mac suddenly found himself sitting on the floor of the Sea King and was looking up at a crewman who was signalling him to move to one of the seats. As soon as he sat down a headset was passed to him.

"Welcome aboard, Sir. We'll be in Aberdeen in 25 minutes."

"Thanks," Mac said. He looked out of the window to get his last glimpse of HMS Herald as she swung around to head back towards the Norwegian Sea.

Since the theft he had felt some excitement in his life again. He wondered what would be next.

CHAPTER TWENTY-SIX
19th June 1990, Kyle of Lochalsh, Scottish Highlands

The radio started to crackle, building into a loud hiss. The passenger in the car fiddled with it, changing channels, altering the volume. Finally he thumped it with his hand.

"What the hell is wrong with it?"

"No point in giving it a wallop, it's not just that one is it? Our personal ones are doing it as well."

"There's every point. It's pissing me off, and it makes me feel better."

The police panda car was on a routine patrol around the Kyle of Lochalsh area. Kyle was busy at this time of year. The Isle of Skye was across the water. Two open-deck car ferries, MVs Lochalsh and Kyleakin, carried tourists and locals alike on the five-minute crossing to the largest of the Inner Hebridean Islands.

"I reported it yesterday while you were off. Seems it's everywhere. HQ was flooded with phone calls from pretty much all the region. They're wondering if it's atmospheric."

"Atmospheric? You mean the aliens are invading?"

"Aye, every day. They get on the ferry and bugger off to Skye," the officer said nodding towards the slipway full of waiting cars.

"Not those aliens, you wally."

"The Comms Department is working on it."

"I wish someone would get their finger out. We're going to miss something juicy if they don't."

"Juicy? Such as?"

"Och, you never know what might happen. There may be a gang from Glasgow tunnelling into the bank as we speak."

"They've obviously set their sights low if they think our bank is worth tunnelling into."

The background noise stopped as abruptly as it had started.

"There you go. That's the sound you get when someone's got their finger out."

"Aye an' next you'll be telling me Brigadoon is real."

"Aye. It's just doon the road."

The noise erupted from the speakers once again. Twice as bad as it had been.

"Bloody marvellous!"

CHAPTER TWENTY-SEVEN
19th June 1990, Peterhead, Aberdeenshire

Once again they were gathered in the incident room at Peterhead police station. Mac stood in front of a blackboard on which everything known about the theft was written. The board was mainly black.

"Right, gentlemen. It would seem our villains sold us a dummy here. The Royal Navy tell us there are no helicopters lying on the bottom anywhere in that area, so let's gather our thoughts. Who, where and why?"

"We're a little further on with the who, Sir," said DS Grant, "or more precisely, the who not. All the Bond pilots have alibis for the night in question. Most were at home with family, one is in the Caribbean, lucky sod, and the rest are offshore."

"That gives us another headache, Alan. If it wasn't one of their pilots then we have a much wider field to look at now. Are there any persons unaccounted for?"

"Just one from Longside, Sir. Stephen Hayling, an engineer. Apparently he goes fishing a lot over on the west coast. When he isn't doing that he's usually off on a motorbike somewhere. No previous for anything other than the odd speeding ticket."

"And where is he now?"

"As far as we know he's away fishing with a mate of his, Andrew Mannion. He's an engineer on a flight simulator in Aberdeen. Again no previous."

"Flight simulator? Could he learn to fly a helicopter in that?"

"I don't know, Sir."

DI Kerr said, "I'll look into the possibility."

"You just want a shot, Sir," quipped DC Alexander.

"Rank has its privileges, Iain. When you get to be a big boy like me, you can play with the big boys' toys too."

A false cough came from the back of the room, loud enough for DI Kerr to hear. There were a few chuckles and muttered comments.

Kerr looked around over the top of his glasses. It made him appear menacing. The room quietened.

He used the same technique when questioning suspects, and had elicited quite a few confessions with only his stare.

"I take it this chap...Hayling, has a key to the hangar then?"

"Yes, Sir. All the engineers have access," replied Grant.

"So he could have brought it out for someone to fly away? When does he get back?"

"He's away until Friday, and then he's back on a day shift."

"Okay, I want someone at his house to keep an eye on it. Same goes for Mannion. I want to know when they return. We can't rule them out of being involved in some way at this stage."

"Could it be smugglers?" asked DC Forbes. "Apparently it's quite common in the States to steal helicopters and aircraft."

"It's possible, but I haven't heard of anything in this part of the world. That in itself leads us back to a where and why," said Mac. "Apart from knowing where it isn't, we don't have any idea where it might have gone. We don't have the time to eliminate all the places where it isn't. We need to pin this down and find where it is. I've had a call from DCI Harris in Northern. There are a couple of reports of helicopters at roughly the right time. I'll be going up there tomorrow first thing to follow it up. Any other ideas as to who?"

Mac looked around but all he saw was a few shakes of the head. "Okay, let's try to think of where."

"We know they flew out to sea first. Maybe they're still there. They could have landed on a ship, Sir," said DI Kerr.

"A possibility, Graham. Robbie, can you get on to that? See if you can find out what ship movements there were around that time. I know it's almost as bad as helicopter movements around here, but we need to start somewhere."

Robbie nodded.

"There's nothing from any of the radars. Makes you wonder why we have radar if no one is going to look at it. At the moment, we only know where it isn't, and have a possible sighting up north. What about the why? Brian, did you find out about the art stuff?"

"Nothing that would be considered high value, Sir. A few exhibitions but everything would be worth less than the helicopter itself."

"There is always that possibility," said Mac. "Maybe they're not using it for anything, but stealing it to sell. Where would you sell a stolen helicopter?"

"That could bring us back to drugs or arms smuggling," said DS Kerr. "It could be sold on to someone wanting to smuggle something into the country."

"You look into that possibility, Alan," Mac said to DS Grant. "Did Governor Coyle say much?"

"He said if there was going to be a break-out then pretty much any of them could be the target. He was wondering if the Home Office would authorise an anti-aircraft gun."

There was a ripple of laughter around the room.

"The thought of anyone having any type of gun in that place, no matter how big it is, does not appeal to me at all. One of the scrotes would find a way to use it," Mac continued. "Our friends in Special Branch have been talking to some gentlemen in trench coats, from somewhere in London, about the offshore installations."

The movie cliché description for secret service personnel brought a few smiles. All that cloak and dagger stuff wasn't their thing. Fingers on collars is what they wanted.

"The general feeling is an attack is possible but not probable. The helicopter only carries four people plus the pilot. If they were armed they could take over an installation, but it would be risky for them. We're not discounting it altogether though, and the radar, which has done so well in ignoring them so far, is on alert to watch for unknown traffic heading to any of the installations. As you can imagine, this is no easy task with the amount of helicopter traffic. The SBS has moved a squadron to Arbroath, just in case. They and the SAS are available if any other threat comes to light. It seems the lady in Number 10 can get things moving when we can't. The consensus is they would have heard something if there was a terrorist attack in the pipeline."

Mac stared at the blackboard.

"So the only thing we know at the moment is a helicopter has been stolen, by person or persons unknown. We've no idea where it's gone, or why it was stolen. If we knew any one of those elements, it might give us a clue to the others. Apart from being fairly sure it's not at the bottom of the North Sea, we don't seem to be much further on than we were Sunday. Our priority now, gentlemen, is to find that helicopter."

CHAPTER TWENTY-EIGHT
19th June 1990, Ceannacroc, Scottish Highlands

The Strathclyde Police Bolkow gleamed under the lights in its makeshift hangar. The paintwork was mainly white with a Day-Glo orange stripe edged in blue. Underneath the stripe at the back of the helicopter on each side were the words 'Police' in large black letters, and just above these 'Strathclyde' was written in small black letters. A small police sign was on the panel just under the nose. Positioned on the diagonal part of the Day-Glo stripe was the Strathclyde Police logo. G-SPOL written in black on the tail-boom, just forward of the VOR/LOC antennas, confirmed the identity of the aircraft.

This Bolkow was in the barn in the Highlands, and not in the hangar at the Glasgow heliport, adjacent to the SECC. The lighting was being provided by a small, quiet-running, petrol generator.

Steve and Andy had needed the best part of the day to repaint the helicopter in its new colours.

"Looks good," Andy said.

"Aye, if you don't look too closely," said Steve, laughing.

"It only has to fool all of the people for some of the time," Andy responded. "Where did you come across this stuff?"

The paint they had used was a special formula, often used in the film world to quickly change the colour of a car or aeroplane. Once the scene had been shot the paint could be removed with nothing more than soap and water.

"I was involved with a privately operated Gazelle. Some company had hired it to produce a drama about a European conflict. The Gazelle was silver and they needed it to be green camo. Was a doddle to put on, but needed a bit of a scrub to get it off. They used the Land Rover too, as a UN vehicle. Got a few quid from that."

"Well, as long as it stays on if it rains."

"It's not going to rain. I don't fancy gadding about in these mountains in cloud." Steve exclaimed. "Bad enough with all of the downdrafts as it is."

Steve had only found out a couple of days before the theft that Strathclyde Police had recently taken delivery of a replacement Bolkow. They had nearly painted this one up in the old colour scheme. Whilst the basic livery was the same, the layout was slightly different. On the other hand only an aircraft spotter probably would have noticed. Still, it was often the smallest of details that resulted in the largest of disasters.

"Good thing they didn't change the base colour."

"I'm sure we would have got away with it," Andy replied.

"Aye, mebbe."

"Well, I don't know about you, but I'm whacked. I think we need a cuppa and something to eat."

"What you cooking today?" asked Steve.

"Oh I thought a nice lobster thermidor with a salad Niçoise and starter of crudités."

"Oh aye, and what are we actually having?"

"Boil in the bag rice."

They laughed. "If this goes to plan," Steve said, "we can have the lobster for breakfast every day."

"Nah, would still want my buttery and a bacon roll."

They had set up a camp nearby in a hollow on the edge of a forest. It was an hour and a half walk, or a twenty minute drive in the Land Rover, but they felt it was worth the effort to be away from the helicopter, in case someone did stumble across it. It was a risk whilst they were there, but the least signs of habitation they left, the harder it would be for the police to associate them with the helicopter, should it ever be discovered. They were careful to take everything with them when they left for the night and the Land Rover was always kept in the barn until they needed it. They had a good sweep around with binoculars each time before leaving, and waited until most hill walkers would be back at their bases swapping stories about the day's walking and the sights they had seen.

This was to be their last night camping out. Tomorrow was the big day. The Land Rover had been moved to a spot near the road for the morning, carefully hidden and covered with a camouflage net. In the morning they would walk to the helicopter with the camping gear. They had left their flying kit in the boot, a chance they had to take for this one night. They didn't want to carry too much in the morning, along with their camping gear.

Andy set up the stove and brought a pan of water to the boil for their gourmet boil in the bag meal. Steve pored over the maps once again, by the light of a shaded torch. As before, the Decca map had the route marked, to and from their goal, but again the primary navigation was going to be looking outside. Andy would do the navigation this time, leaving Steve to concentrate on the flying. The advantage was the flight would be in daylight.

"You know it's not too late for us to walk away," said Steve.

"Do you want to?" asked Andy.

"No, I'm just saying we could just leave it. It could go horribly wrong tomorrow. We could end up as some hairy lifer's blow-up doll for the next few years. Well, maybe not you, I'm the one with the looks. Or we could end up dead."

Andy laughed. "I think I would prefer the latter if I had a choice. You know it'll be fine. We've planned this to the last detail. So unless you fly us into the hillside, I don't see a problem."

"The timing, Andy, it's so critical to this. It has to be spot on. And not all of that is in our hands. That's what worries me."

"I'm sure it'll all fall into place. I have to admit it would've been nice to practice it. Bit of a giveaway if we had done."

"What did you say, officer?" Steve chuckled, speaking to an imaginary police officer behind Andy. "Oh the helicopter. Yes, we're just having a practice run to check the timing of our little escapade. Pay us no mind, we'll soon have it out of the way."

They both laughed.

"So we still go?" asked Steve.

"Oh aye. Might as well get hung for a sheep as a lamb. Two thefts are better than one."

"Okay, that's settled then. How's that lobster coming on?"

"Ready in two minutes. Will Sir be having the Bollinger?"

"Indeed he will, Jeeves," said Steve.

"Soon," said Andy, "as long as the timing is right. In the meantime a cup of tea will have to suffice."

CHAPTER TWENTY-NINE
19th June 1990, Victoria Embankment, London

The Daimler limousine came to a halt on the double yellow lines, across from the entrance to the Tattershall Castle. The darkened windows prevented Harry from seeing into the back of the car, but he recognised Lenny in the front passenger seat. He had never seen the driver before.

Harry had been waiting for the past ten minutes for Munro to collect him. The arrangement was to meet here, then for Munro to take Harry and Lenny to Heathrow, in time to catch the afternoon flight to Inverness.

Harry carried a pilot's flight bag in one hand and a small bag over one shoulder. They planned on coming back the next day and he liked to travel light.

The pilot's case was for carrying the money. His contribution was already in the case. He had suggested a flight bag to Munro, they were small enough to take on as hand luggage, and attracted little attention. Aircrew positioned to another base on flights all the time and Harry might be mistaken for another positioning pilot. As long as they didn't weigh his bag. With all that money it would be well over the cabin baggage limit. The trick was to make it seem light when checking in. He didn't want that amount of cash going in the hold. Munro had readily agreed and said he would place his contribution in the case on the way to the airport.

The rear passenger window slid down and Munro's unmistakable voice said, "In you get, Clark. We don't want to be getting a parking ticket now do we?"

Harry opened the door and climbed in. He was with the lion again, not quite in his den, but near enough. It made him nervous.

Munro seemed totally relaxed. "Cigar, Clark? Finest Cuban."

"Ah... no thanks, Donald."

"Drink then perhaps? A sort of pre-deal celebration." Munro indicated the small but well-stocked mini-bar in front of them underneath the glass partition separating them from the two men in the front.

Although Harry wanted to keep his head clear he also wanted to steady his nerves. "Don't mind if I do, Donald," he said, pouring himself a Scotch.

"Well, big day tomorrow. You and I should be well on the way to being even better off if this goes to plan."

"It will."

Munro pointed to a large bag on the floor in front of the folded-up occasional seat. "My contribution is in there. I will let you have the pleasure of packing it in the flight bag. Half a million in cash and two million in bearer bonds. Please try not to spend it all, Clark. I really would like some change on this deal."

Harry laughed. "You already know my negotiating skills. I'll come back with as much of this as I can."

"Indeed I do, Clark, Indeed I do."

After Harry transferred the money, they said little for the rest of the journey; each man deep in his own thoughts.

They pulled up outside Terminal 1 departures. As soon as the car had stopped, Lenny was out and opening the back door.

Munro reached out to shake Harry's hand.

"I know you won't need it but good luck, Clark."

"Thank you Donald, I'll do my best."

"You will indeed."

Harry reached for the flight bag as he went to step out of the car, and Donald caught his hand in a tight grip. Harry froze.

"Ah...I think you are forgetting something."

Harry cocked his head on one side in a question.

"Lenny carries that from now on."

"Ah, of course," said Harry, nodding.

Munro let go of his hand and Lenny reached in to take the case.

Lenny too had a small shoulder bag. On Lenny this looked almost like an overgrown handbag. Harry could see why he would be a handy man to have around when you needed some muscle.

They passed through the doors to the terminal building and Harry looked up at the flight announcement board to check their flight. DA156 13:40 departure for Inverness was checking in now. They made their way to the check-in desk.

"Just me and you now," said Harry.

Lenny looked at him, looked around the terminal building and frowned.

"Not literally," said Harry.

The frown deepened.

Now Harry was beginning to see what Munro had meant. The lion was on his way back to his den, and now Harry was heading off to the Highlands with the orang-utan. He suspected a real orang-utan would be slightly better in the conversation stakes. This was going to be so much fun.

CHAPTER THIRTY
19th June 1990, Inverness, Scotland

Nicky headed off to interview a farmer who had telephoned the paper with a possible sighting of the helicopter. In need of a drink and a call of nature he called into Inverness Airport. He was drinking his coffee when he saw what he thought was a familiar figure walking out from the arrival hall. Sure enough it was Lenny, a kid he knew from his schooldays in the East End. Last he'd heard he was working for Donald Munro. What on earth was he doing in this part of the world?

This might be more worthy of his time than interviewing the farmer who had probably seen a military helicopter anyway. He gulped down the last of his coffee and discreetly tagged along behind Lenny. Lenny stopped at the car hire desk with a companion and Nicky got a glimpse of the second man. He tried to recollect where he had seen him before.

Inverness Airport was not the sort of place you could lose yourself in a crowd. Regional airports never were. Nicky averted his gaze and lowered his head as he passed the two men and headed out of the building towards his car. He had left his car in the car park in front of the terminal and he could keep an eye out for them as they emerged. His nose twitched. He could smell a story in here somewhere. He decided to follow them.

Irritated by the familiarity of Lenny's companion, he racked his brains. He recognised him from somewhere but for the life of him he couldn't remember where. It would come to him and when it did he was sure it would be the key to whatever it was the two of them were up to.

Nicky had the motor running ready to follow, and it wasn't long before Lenny and his companion emerged from the building walking towards the hire cars.

Lenny carried a bag similar to those carried by pilots. Nicky was pretty certain Lenny hadn't taken up flying for a living. He couldn't think of a reason why he would be in Inverness either. It wasn't anywhere near his boss's old stomping ground, so unless Munro was now in the oil construction business, which Nicky doubted, there was nothing obvious to bring him this far north.

A narrow and twisting lane led from the airport to the main road, this was not Heathrow after all. He hung back a little but couldn't afford to let them get too far ahead. He needed to know whether they would turn towards Nairn or Inverness when they reached the main road. Even then he still might lose them as it wasn't always easy getting out onto the A96. The car in front signalled a right turn towards Inverness. The back of his mind was itching to tell him where he knew the other guy from. Unfortunately, the itch was just too far out of reach to scratch.

It surprised Nicky when they carried on through the city and picked up the A82. They had passed through the largest urban area. Apart from Fort William to the West there was little else. As for the North, he was sure he'd seen 'here be dragons' marked on a map one time. The city boy didn't like the idea of being so far away from civilisation. His surprise deepened when they turned off onto a road signposted to Kyle of Lochalsh. That really was heading into dragon territory.

After another thirty minutes or so of trying to pretend he wasn't behind them, the car in front pulled up outside a pub, or to be more exact an inn, as the sign outside corrected him. This made no sense at all. Nicky pulled into the car park across the road where he had a clear view of the parked car and the entrance. After three hours of sitting in the car he resigned himself to the fact they were probably staying the night. Great. He couldn't chance booking a room for himself as the odds were too high he'd be spotted by Lenny. In any case, cooped up in a room meant he wouldn't see if they left to go somewhere else. Nothing for it but to spend the night in a car on some godforsaken moor in dragon territory. Not a great prospect to look forward to, given the countryside scared the shit out of him. All that screeching and rustling gave him the shivers. "Best lock the doors," he thought as he hunkered down for the night.

CHAPTER THIRTY-ONE
20th June 1990, Ceannacroc, Scottish Highlands

This was not good. Steve needed his rest, but sleep wouldn't come. They were a few hours away from a life-changing event. One that would need all his concentration. Instead he was lying awake going over everything, wondering what they had missed. And he was sure there was something.

All the self-doubts were creeping in now. He knew it was a strange time for them to surface. After all, the theft had gone without a hitch. Well, almost. The getaway plan was in place. Andy knew exactly what he was supposed to do and was more than capable of doing it. So why the doubts?

He went over it in his mind again and again. An endless cycle of doubt, questioning, checking the plans and confirming, followed by the doubt again. It wasn't a lack of planning, it was a lack of confidence. People were relying on him. They always did. He was flattered by their faith and scared by it too. Though he rarely failed at whatever it was he turned his hand to, others had far more confidence in his abilities than he had.

A fraud. That's what he felt he was, and one day someone would find him out. Maybe that day would be tomorrow. Maybe this was a step, a big step, too far.

One-forty. God, he needed to get some sleep. How could he turn off these thoughts? He gently rolled back the sleeping bag and quietly slid open the zip on the tent. He stepped out into the still air and looked up. Stars were visible, even in a sky not truly dark. How could anyone see nature like this and not be amazed? He let out a big sigh. After tomorrow he may never see this again. He might be dead or locked up. Either way he would not be looking at a starry sky.

Come on Steve, snap out of it. Get your head down and sleep. Put your doubts behind you and get on with it. He slipped back into the sleeping bag. This time the sleep came.

CHAPTER THIRTY-TWO
20th June 1990, Cluanie Inn, Scottish Highlands

Nicky woke with a start. He took a few moments to work out where he was and why he had such a sore neck. Then he remembered he was in a car in the middle of nowhere, the sore neck a result of having his head jammed against the window. Across the road he could make out the car Lenny and the unknown man had arrived in. That was a bonus. They hadn't disappeared while Nicky had been asleep. He checked his watch. Oh you've got to be kidding; one forty-five.

He became aware of another area of pain. He desperately needed to answer a call of nature. Oh well nothing for it, he would have to chance the wildlife he was sure surrounded his car, waiting to devour him as soon as he stepped out. He was about to open the door when he remembered the interior light. No sense in giving the game away now to anyone, or anything that may be watching. He reached and moved the switch to the off position, then opened the door.

The first thing that struck him was how eerily quiet it was. He expected to hear all kinds of wild creatures. Just because they were quiet didn't mean they weren't there. Nicky dashed around the back of the car and relieved himself as quickly as possible. He was sure the sound of the water hitting the undergrowth would summon every predator for miles around. Were there bears in Scotland? He couldn't remember. The distinctive call of a Tawny Owl broke the silence, echoing in the valley. Nicky almost wet himself. How could people live in places like this?

Nature answered, he settled down to continue his wait. He rummaged around in his bag to see what he had to eat, more importantly what he had in the way of drinks. He was rewarded with a half-eaten bar of chocolate and an almost full bottle of Coke. A veritable feast at this time of day.

He broke off a square of chocolate and started to run through all the things he thought Lenny and partner might be up to in this part of the world. It took him all of thirty-seconds. He could not think of anything that would interest them here. The answer to whatever they were doing, he was sure would lie in London. In the meantime he would have to stick close to them, but not too close.

Damn. Nicky realised he hadn't checked in with his boss. He'd be wondering where the hell he had got to. Good thing there was a call box outside the Inn. There would be someone on the news desk so he could call in and leave a message. He was unlikely to be seen by anyone in the Inn at this hour. The bears? Now, that was something else.

CHAPTER THIRTY-THREE
20th June 1990, Inverness, Scotland

"I can't get a handle on this noise, Larry. It's on all our frequencies and it comes and goes. It seems to be on all the repeaters too."

Despite trying hard, Gordon could not get to the bottom of the noise plaguing Northern Constabulary's communications.

For the past two days an intermittent static noise had blocked out transmissions over the entire area, and so far they had not found the source. To say the Chief was not happy was an understatement.

"The thing that puzzles me is that it's on all the channels. I could understand it being on one, but all?"

Larry shrugged his shoulders. "I'm not far enough up the food chain to worry about that. I fix the radios. That stuff's your job."

"Yeah, yeah. You're never going to get on if you don't get involved in the network stuff."

"I fix radios. I don't understand all that crap. Give me a broken radio and I'm fine, but all that switching stuff, it's magic to me."

Larry actually understood it very well, but as the job really didn't have any promotion prospects anyway, he didn't see any reason to help Gordon. Dead men's shoes was the only way he would get promoted. Let him struggle.

Larry knew Gordon wasn't as clever as he thought, and that knowledge had allowed him to put his little box where it was. He had inserted a white noise generator circuit into the force's transmitters. Whenever he wanted, the generator would transmit white noise on all frequencies. And Gordon would never find it because every time he looked like he was getting close, Larry turned it off. What really amused Larry was he had the control box right in front of him, on the bench, and Gordon was none the wiser. His head was so far up his own arse he wasn't aware of what was around him. Larry knew it wasn't enough to block the outgoing transmissions. He needed to block the incoming calls too. That was what was puzzling Gordon. The radios worked on a duplex system, transmitting on one frequency, receiving on a different one. The box on the roof of the Kyle police station was doing its job. He was controlling it from here. Each burst of noise from here had a code inserted into it. The box in Kyle would receive and process it. The code changed the state of the noise generator in Kyle. The first code would switch it on and the second switch it off again, and so on. Larry could completely stop the radio communications of the Northern Constabulary right from his bench.

Once this was all over, he would quietly disappear to some sunny island in the Med and not have a care in the world. He would remove the noise generator before he went, but the box at Kyle would have to stay. There was nothing to trace that back to him anyway. He had been careful not to touch anything with his bare hands when assembling it and the components had been bought in London by someone else, and mailed to him. He mailed it back to them and someone had fitted it in Kyle. He didn't know who had done what, nor did he care. What he would earn from this would see him through to old age.

He couldn't wait.

CHAPTER THIRTY-FOUR
20th June 1990, Ceannacroc, Scottish Highlands

Andy became aware of something annoying him. Sunlight shining through the tent, that's what it was. He looked at his watch.

"Steve. Wake up. We've overslept."

Steve stirred then bolted upright. "What time is it?"

"Nine-thirty. Get your arse out of there. We're going to miss it if we don't get a move on. Guess breakfast is out of the window now."

Steve thought for a moment. "No, we need to eat. I don't know when we'll get chance after this. We need to keep our blood sugar up. I'll strike camp and load the rucksacks, you get on with breakfast."

Andy grabbed the stove and set to preparing bacon, eggs and a pot of tea. As usual, Steve was right. How come he seemed to think of everything?

Twenty minutes later there was an empty camp, save for two guys eating bacon and eggs and sipping tea from two large mugs. They were still behind schedule but not dangerously so. They had a five mile hike along the track to reach the barn. It would take them an hour and a half at a fast pace. This would leave them only half an hour to get the helicopter ready to go.

Good thing Steve had insisted they pack everything away last night or else they would be struggling.

"What happened to the alarm?" Andy asked.

"I must have forgotten to set it. I wonder what else I've forgotten."

"Steve will you pack it in. You haven't forgotten anything. We've been over it time and time again. There's nothing that's been missed. I bet if we were in an earthquake zone you would have covered that too."

"I have covered that."

"Really?"

"No, you teuchter, of course I haven't."

Steve laughed.

"That's better. You're laughing."

"Aye you're right. If I stay all wound up I'll screw something up. You have a quick scout round make sure I've not missed packing anything."

Andy wandered around the camping area for a couple of minutes.

"Apart from where we put the tent I don't see anything. And rough camping isn't unusual around here so I don't suppose anyone will notice it. In any case a few days and it won't even show."

"Right. Let's get to it then." Steve said, hoisting his rucksack and tent on his back, and with that they set off.

CHAPTER THIRTY-FIVE
20th June 1990, Cluanie Inn, Scottish Highlands

The Cluanie Inn situated on the western end of Loch Cluanie and nestling between the munros, had originally been built as a resting place for the highland cattle drovers on their way to market. The inn was now a base for tourists to explore the area, particularly hill walkers. As Harry approached the reception desk, an attractive young woman looked up from her work and smiled at him.

"Good afternoon, Sir, is there something I can help you with?"

This was a different receptionist to the one who had checked them in the night before.

"Hello. When I checked in last night I mentioned to the receptionist I needed a room for a meeting today. Will there be one available please?"

"Mr Hart?" she asked, after checking the diary.

"Yes."

"Yes, the lounge is ready for you. Would you like some refreshments brought in?" She had a soft Highland lilt to her voice.

"We're not quite ready yet, but thank you. We're waiting for someone to arrive. He should be here soon."

"Would you like me to call your room when he gets here?"

"I'm expecting a Mr Silva. Yes, please, that would be great."

The receptionist wrote down the name on a post-it note.

"Is there anything else I can help you with?"

Harry thanked her and went back to his room. This was all going too well, he didn't know why, but he was feeling uneasy. He was regretting the choice of location. Although he had been to this area before, he did not feel as confident as in London. He knew his way around the capital. He felt safe there.

He went over things once again in his mind. If this went to plan, they were going to be wealthy. He hoped the diamonds lived up to expectations. If not, he would have egg on his face and a lot of explaining to do to someone who didn't listen to explanations. Perhaps his unease was because his temporary business partner had a reputation for not being the most understanding of people when things didn't go his way.

He looked out over the loch. It was a beautiful place to spend a holiday. He lay on the bed and stared at the ceiling. This was going to be a turning point in his life.

Twenty minutes later the phone startled him. He had drifted off.

"Hello?"

"Hello Mr Hart, your guests are here."

"There's more than one?"

"Yes. Mr Silva has another gentleman with him."

"Thank you. I'll be right along."

The unease Harry had been feeling developed into downright nervousness. He couldn't put his finger on the reason. He hadn't expected a second person and had assumed Silva would be alone. But there was no reason why there shouldn't be someone with him.

It wasn't as if Harry was a newcomer to this game, having lost his diamond deal virginity when he was in his teens. His father had allowed him a free hand in his first deal, and he had done amazingly well.

His second one lost quite an amount of money and taught him a valuable lesson. These days he kept his eyes on the diamonds at all times. No one would switch them on him ever again. If Harry bought them, Harry put them back in the bag himself, or whatever container they had arrived in. He had done countless deals like this one. Well, maybe not quite like this one. A remote inn in the wilds of Scotland was a first for him.

He left the room and walked along the corridor to Lenny's door and knocked.

"Yeah?"

"They're here."

"Right."

Lenny came out of the room still pulling on his jacket one-handed and carrying the flight-bag in the other. Harry got a clear view of the shoulder holster and blanched. He was no longer nervous. He was scared.

Completely oblivious to Harry's stare, Lenny set off towards reception with Harry in tow. Harry now knew what had been in the packet Lenny had collected from reception when they arrived last night. Munro must have called in a favour from someone north of the border to provide Lenny with his weapon after the flight.

Two gentlemen waited in the reception area. They were clearly of African origin, with dark skin, which seemed slightly incongruous in the Scottish Highlands.

Harry stepped forward, "Mr Silva?" looking at each of the men in turn.

"Mr Hart, I presume?" Ollie reached out and they shook hands.

Harry caught a flash of something in the other man's eyes, like a warning.

"Mr Hart please let me introduce you to my...ah ...associate, Mr Pereira. He is providing the security for the diamonds."

Harry shook hands with Mr Pereira and tried to weigh him up. He was smartly dressed but clearly ill-at-ease in his surroundings. He had an odd mixture of nervousness tinged with arrogance about him. Harry was sure this man would normally be self-assured. Perhaps bringing them to the Highlands was not a bad idea after all.

He introduced Lenny to the newcomers and explained Lenny had much the same role as Mr Pereira. He turned to the receptionist and asked her to bring some drinks through to the lounge. They all settled on tea, with the exception of Lenny who wanted a Coke.

They stepped into the lounge and closed the door. It would not be a good idea for other guests to catch sight of the diamonds spread out on the table. Harry suggested to Ollie the two winged-back chairs over to one side of the window would be the ideal place for them to sit. An old occasional table separated the chairs.

Lenny and Pereira seated themselves at the opposite ends of a chesterfield sofa, studiously avoiding each other's gaze.

"We'll wait for the refreshments before we begin, Mr Silva. Good journey?"

"Very pleasant, Mr Hart. I have not seen such scenery before. I have visited London many times but this is such a spectacular place. It is hard to believe it is the same country."

"The Scottish people would give you an argument about it being the same country," Harry said, laughing.

There was a knock at the door. Harry opened it and the tray of drinks and biscuits was brought in by the young woman. She set it down on the coffee table in front of the chesterfield.

"Is there anything else I can get for you?"

Harry declined and she left the room, closing the door behind her.

Harry and Ollie poured themselves their tea and then went back to their winged-back chairs.

"So, Mr Silva, you have some quality pieces I believe."

"I do indeed, Mr Hart. I think you will be most impressed." He signalled for Pereira to bring over the case he was protecting like a small child.

Harry spread a small black cloth over the table. He produced a loupe from his pocket. Ollie waited until Pereira had set the combinations on the attaché case locks and opened it, so Ollie could remove the black bag from inside. Pereira returned to his seat but his gaze never left the pair at the table.

Ollie had just tipped out the contents of the bag when there was a knock on the door.

It was the receptionist again.

"Sorry to bother you, and I am not sure this will make any sense, but I've had a phone call from the police. They say they've had a tip off there is some sort of deal taking place here, and a gang is on the way to commit a robbery..."

Lenny jumped up as he heard the word 'robbery' and reached into his jacket.

Startled, the receptionist stopped mid-sentence and stepped back.

Harry put his hand up to Lenny and shook his head.

At Lenny's movement, Pereira leapt to his feet and moved to the table, where the diamonds were in full view.

"Go on, please," Harry said.

The receptionist continued, "I really have no idea what they were talking about but they said you would understand Mr Hart. Apparently the gang has been under observation for some time."

"I'm not sure what they are talking about either."

"They gave me a number you can call. Ask for this officer."

She handed Harry a piece of paper and continued, "You can use the phone on the reception desk. Dial 9 for an outside line."

Harry glanced at Lenny, the money and the diamonds then went with the receptionist to the phone and dialled.

CHAPTER THIRTY-SIX
20th June 1990, Inverness, Scotland

It was mid-morning when Mac arrived at Northern Constabulary HQ in Inverness. Rather than discuss the helicopter theft on the phone, he had elected to drive up to discuss things face to face with his opposite number. It was a good chance to catch up anyway. Mac and DCI Harris had known each other for some time, having met on a training course at the National Police College at Kincardine.

"Mac. How are you?" Mac and the DCI shook hands.

"Surviving, Brian, surviving."

"Aye. Aren't we all?"

DCI Harris led Mac through to his office. "Drink?"

"Aye a coffee please, white no sugar."

Harris picked up his phone.

"Dougie, could you do me a favour and bring up a couple of coffees, white no sugar. Aye, that'd be great. Thanks, Dougie."

"So you have yourself a bit of a headache there, Mac."

"Tell me about it. Got the Chief breathing down my neck, and he has the Home Office breathing down his. The only things we know for sure are it's missing, and it didn't go down in the sea as we first suspected. We had a bit of luck there. There was a Navy survey ship heading north. The Navy agreed to let us use it for twenty-four hours. Monday afternoon they started a search. No sign of anything unusual was found, so we're fairly certain it was a decoy."

Harris grimaced as Mac continued.

"The latest thinking is they came up here. As I said when I called you, we've had a few people responding to the appeal saying they heard an aircraft early Sunday morning. We checked with the military. Lossie had a Sea King up for a medical tasking at Loch Torridon, which might account for it, but in one of the reports the caller believes there might have been two aircraft."

"I take it if the Sea King was going to the Torridon area, then these reports are from the north of the Moray Firth too. It's a vast area to search. Lots of valleys and forests they could hide in. You name it we have it. They could be anywhere in the Highlands."

"It doesn't have the range to be too far north, not if it was flown out to sea to arrange the decoy first. The Bond pilots reckon they'd have to be somewhere in the southern part of the Highlands, if they're here at all, and the report of a second helicopter might be the key."

"Still gives us a pretty large area to work with, but it's a bit more populated." Harris went to a map on the wall. "Where were these reports from?"

"The first was near Dornoch. A farmer heard an aircraft of some sort, sometime around three in the morning. He thought nothing of it until the TV appeal. It seems to be too far north of where the Sea King would route."

Harris pushed a pin into the map. "Yes, it does. Where was the second one?"

"Evanton. Now the thing about this one is the caller was sure he could see flashing lights to the South but was convinced there was something flying to the North too, only he couldn't see any lights."

"What time was this?"

"Sometime after three again."

"Any others?" asked Harris as he put another pin in the map.

"The last one from Contin near Strathpeffer seems to tie in too. It was timed at three forty-five. This time the helicopter was seen low down but the reporter could not really describe it. Only got a brief glimpse, but he was sure it wasn't yellow so is unlikely to be the Sea King. Apart from which the crew say they cleared Strathpeffer some twenty minutes earlier."

"The caller could have been wrong with his time."

"No. He's adamant about the time. He was up early to drive down to Glasgow for a meeting."

The final pin went in the board and Harris said, "If all these are related then we have a rough direction. Still leaves us a large area to work so let's hope we get another break." Harris paused, "This line is north-east to south-west. Seems a long way round if it was yours, and they were heading for this area."

"We think the debris was meant to hold us up longer, and once they were out to sea they had to fly well to the North to avoid Kinloss and Lossie."

"Why on earth would they want to bring it here?" asked Harris.

"I suppose it would help if we had some idea of who took it, but so far we haven't a clue."

There was a knock at the door. "Come in," said Harris.

A uniformed sergeant entered carrying two mugs of coffee. "Thanks, Dougie. Been any more reports of sightings of the helicopter?"

"Several reports of red helicopters, Sir, as we suspected there would be, but all have turned out to be legitimate flights."

"Thanks, Dougie. Let me know if anything else comes in."

"Sir."

Mac thought for a moment.

"Assuming the flight was kept as straight as possible to conserve fuel, where would be a likely place along the route where they could be heading?"

"Good question well put. The only airfield I can think of within reach would be Plockton, but that would mean swinging west. Of course they don't really need an airfield do they?"

"They need to get fuel from somewhere. They won't have much once they land if they've come this far. You know Bond operate out of Plockton?"

Mac ran his hand through his hair and smiled.

"We have been assured they don't have it there. They say they might have noticed."

The two men laughed.

"So we come back to the question, why here?" Mac said.

"Ah, the billion dollar question. The target, if there is one that is, might not be here. They might think this is a good place to hide until they do whatever it is they're doing."

Mac sighed. "This is getting us nowhere. We need another break in the case."

Brian nodded slowly. "Anyway, Mac, how are you keeping?"

"To be honest, Brian, I think I'm just hanging on. I can take retirement next year and I'm thinking of doing just that, selling up and going somewhere warm."

"Really? I thought you were settled where you are?"

"Too many memories. I need a fresh start."

"Anywhere in mind?"

"No, not really. Not given it that much thought." Mac started to chuckle. "Probably end up in Spain with a bunch of retired criminals."

CHAPTER THIRTY-SEVEN
20th June 1990, Near Cluanie Inn, Scottish Highlands

The man reached for the handset and clamped it to his ear with his shoulder, whilst he dialled. With his free hand he lit the cigarette in his mouth, and waited for his call to be answered.

"Northern Constabulary, how can I help?"

"I thought you might be interested. I saw two fellas standing by a helicopter near Loch Cluanie."

"Can I take your name please caller?"

"No. Sorry. I don't want to be involved. I heard an appeal on the radio a couple of days ago. Thought you might like to know in case this is the one you're looking for."

"Where and when was this?"

"About forty minutes ago. It was about two hundred yards off the A87 in a little depression in the hillside. You couldn't see it from the road. There's a forest track on the north side of the road, about a mile and a half from the Cluanie Inn. They're in there. I haven't heard them leave. I got to a phone box as quick as I could but I'm not built for running."

"Are you sure you can't..." but the caller had already hung up.

He unclipped the handset from the telephone wires, fastened it to his tool belt and started to climb down from the telegraph pole, cigarette in mouth.

He smiled. Let the fun begin.

CHAPTER THIRTY-EIGHT
20th June 1990, Inverness, Scotland

Mac's impending retirement was still the topic of conversation when there was a knock at the door.

"Come in."

Dougie came into the room, "Sir, we've had a sighting of two men and a helicopter at Loch Cluanie."

"How recent?"

"The caller said about forty minutes ago."

"Damn, they could have flown anywhere in that time."

"He said it was on the ground and he hasn't heard it leave."

"Who called it in?"

"Wouldn't leave any details, Sir. He said it was near the Cluanie Inn. Gave us directions, apparently it's off a forest track about a mile and a half to the west of the Inn."

"What do you think, Mac, worth getting a car there eh?"

"We might have to go from here, Sir. We're still having problems with the radios and we can't raise Kyle on the phone."

"Damn. We're at least forty-five minutes away. Dougie, keep trying to raise Kyle, and also Fort William, see if they can get anyone up there. We'll head up there with a couple of Uniforms. Come on, Mac, we'll take my car."

Harris grabbed his car keys from the desk, his coat from a hook by the door and rushed out, Mac following closely behind.

As Harris dashed through the headquarters he shouted to a couple of startled uniformed officers to follow him. They exchanged glances, the puzzlement obvious on their faces.

"Don't just bloody stand there like a couple of highland virgins at a ceilidh, get your bloody arses in gear, get a car, and follow me."

That had the desired effect, and the officers followed Harris and Mac out of the door.

Harris fired out of the HQ car park, Mac still struggling to put on his seat belt.

"Hell, Brian, give a body a chance to get strapped in."

"No time to lose. This is the best sighting we've had yet. Even if we don't get them, we might find evidence at the landing site. At least we know what area they're in now."

"Aye, but we don't know why."

"True. I can't think of any reason they would be in that area unless they're stealing trees, heather or hill walkers."

"What about Eilean Donan? Anything going on there?"

"Not as far as I'm aware. Unless there is an exhibition of some sort, there would be nothing high value there."

The A82 clings tenaciously to the side of Loch Ness, twisting and undulating along the shoreline. There were not many opportunities for overtaking, even though traffic was lighter than in the city, so Harris made his own opportunities where he could. Summer tourists, often oblivious to the traffic around them whilst taking in the sights were no exception today, even when the traffic had two tone sirens and flashing blue lights. Harris used plenty of words to make even a squaddie blush. Mac hung on in the front seat, too scared to take his eyes off the road for even a glance at the famous Loch.

"Remind me again where you came in the advanced driving class," he asked Harris.

"Did I do one?"

"Apparently not," replied Mac.

He risked a glance over his shoulder and was surprised to see the marked police car was keeping up with them.

"Err...just a thought, Brian. Shouldn't we let the marked car take the lead?"

"What and miss all the fun? Not on your life. Sit back and enjoy."

"Yeah. Just let me know when the fun part starts will ya?"

It was another fifteen miles before they reached Invermoriston. They would leave the side of Loch Ness here and start the long ascent towards the Cluanie pass.

As they turned off the main road, Mac noted the startled expression of the British Telecom engineer, who had been disturbed getting something from the back of his van, parked outside the Glenmoriston telephone exchange. Mac gave him a wave as they passed.

"Got to keep the natives happy," he said to Harris.

CHAPTER THIRTY-NINE
20th June 1990, Ceannacroc, Scottish Highlands

The radio crackled. "Home run, home run."

"Time to go," said Steve.

Steve and Andy were dressed as Strathclyde Police Air Support Unit Officers. They needed to be if this part of the plan was to succeed. No one had to doubt they were genuine police officers. Andy wore sunglasses and an open-face crash helmet on which the word 'POLICE' was painted on the front and back. Steve wore a similar helmet. He wasn't going to be as close to anyone as Andy would be; at least he hoped not. If he came close to anyone, it was likely to be a real police officer.

They opened the barn doors and between them pushed the helicopter out on its ground-handling wheels. As before when Steve stole the helicopter, the wheels were removed and put in the boot. They had spent some time making sure nothing was left in the barn, but Andy had one last look whilst Steve started the helicopter. They didn't want to leave anything that could be traced back to them.

This was a risky time. It was early afternoon and a bright summer day. The hills would be full of walkers and it was more than likely someone would see them taking the helicopter from its hiding place. Even if they didn't, the noise would certainly attract the attention of anyone within earshot.

They lifted off and headed west.

"Bugger, walkers off to the right. The cat's out of the bag now."

"As long as they aren't here when we return," answered Andy. "Then it might be a tad difficult getting away."

Their route followed a series of shallow valleys until they dropped down into the western end of Glen Affric. Still flying west, they entered Glean Lichd, eventually coming out of the valley at Kintail, where they picked up the A87 main road to Kyle of Lochalsh.

Andy breathed a sigh of relief. "God, I'm glad that's over."

"Oh I don't know, flying in the valleys is kind of fun."

"Aye for you, but you weren't navigating."

"Well, you can relax now. Even you can follow a road."

"If you weren't flying I'd chuck something at you," growled Andy.

Plenty of people could see them now. Summer in this part of the world meant tourists, and they came here in droves; little white faces looking up to watch the helicopter following the road up the hill towards Loch Cluanie. No hiding now, not that they needed to anymore.

A few minutes later the Cluanie Inn was in sight. Steve flew one circuit of the property then made an approach to the car park on the western end of the building. Fortunately, the car park was relatively empty and he aimed at the end furthest away from the Inn.

As Steve had expected, with so many tourists on the road a small crowd formed to watch the helicopter land. However, he doubted anyone would be able to give an accurate description of them because of the flying helmets and the mirrored aviator sunglasses.

The helicopter would be a big distraction. The human mind is easily diverted. Often in armed robberies the victim can describe the gun in detail but not the person holding it. Most of the spectators would be looking at the helicopter and almost oblivious to the people around or inside it.

"Hell, Steve, have we got a problem?"

"No. Why are you...? Oh the shaking. It's only the Bolkow letting us know it's still there. You get used to it. That's why the approach speed was high and we slowed down quickly."

Steve touched down, lowering the collective all the way. He left the engines running at full power. They may need to get off the ground quickly.

"Over to you, Officer Dibble," he said.

"Oh gee thanks, Top Cat." Andy gave him a wave as he slid the door open, jumped out and walked quickly towards the Inn.

As he approached the entrance Andy saw a group of four men waiting outside.

"Are you expecting us?" asked Andy.

"We had a phone call telling us you were on the way. What's going on?" asked a tall, dark-haired man.

"I don't really have time to explain but we have been on the trail of some diamond thieves for some months. Somehow they got to hear about your deal and we believe they're nearby. Unfortunately our nearest ground units are some distance away. We were in the area training when we got the call to come and take care of your valuables until the units arrive."

"I can't say I'm happy letting this lot out of my sight," the tall man said. "And will we be safe? Can you not stay with us?"

"HQ are hoping to get units in place before they arrive and nab them in the attempt. Unfortunately they don't know exactly when the attempt is going to be made. We were given a task and here we are. Look, we really don't have the time to discuss it," said Andy. "Are we going to take them to safety or not?"

"I suppose so," he said reluctantly handing over a large, black flight-bag.

One of the other men handed him a large pouch.

"When will you be back?"

"As soon as we get the all clear," said Andy. "We're going to stand off in the next valley. We've been told to keep out of sight."

CHAPTER FORTY

20th June 1990, Glen Moriston, Scottish Highlands

They were soon out of the village; on a national speed limit road. There was little traffic now; Harris pressed his foot harder on the accelerator to take advantage of the open road and sweeping bends.

Several miles later, he nodded towards the Single Track Road sign.

"Right, Mac. You wanted to know — the fun starts now."

"Wonderful," said Mac gloomily.

"Don't worry, it's only a couple of miles."

"I'm not worried. I need a change of underwear."

Harris laughed as he put on opposite lock to correct a back end skid.

Soon the road opened up again into two lanes. There were far less bends and Harris soon had the car at top speed.

Before long they had reached the junction with the A87 and shortly after, Mac saw the dam that marked the start of Loch Cluanie.

"Not long now," Harris said.

"You talking about the journey or life in general?" retorted Mac.

"Ach, you're a wuss."

"One that has managed to stay alive, up to now."

Harris turned off the two-tone siren, and eased off a little on the accelerator.

"No sense in alerting them if they're still there."

In every lay-by along the shore line, surprised tourists turned to stare as the two police cars sped by.

As they approached a right hand corner Mac saw a sign for the Inn. "How far from the Inn did he say?"

"About a mile and a half."

"I think we should stop there and ask if anyone has heard anything before we spend time looking in the forest."

"Aye, you might be right." Harris slowed down to approach the Inn which was now in sight.

As they pulled up outside the Inn they had a clear view of the lower car park and the police helicopter parked with its rotors turning.

Mac started to get out of the car, and quickly turned back to Harris.

"Did you call Strathclyde for assistance?"

"No."

"It's them," he shouted. "It's the stolen helicopter." He started to run towards a police officer wearing a flying suit, who was walking quickly towards the helicopter.

"Police. Stay where you are," he shouted.

CHAPTER FORTY-ONE
20th June 1990, Cluanie Inn, Scottish Highlands

Andy walked briskly towards the helicopter and was on the edge of the car park when he was aware of a car pulling up behind him. He twisted round in time to see a burly man open the passenger door and step halfway out of the car, pause, and speak to the driver.

He turned back towards Andy and shouted.

"Police. Stay where you are."

Andy broke into a run, hampered slightly by the flight bag. He risked another glance behind and saw the man was now out of the car and running towards him. He looked back at the helicopter and saw Steve was raising the collective making the helicopter light on its skids, creating little dust devils in the car park. He obviously didn't intend to hang around once Andy was inside. Andy glanced over his shoulder again. The gap had reduced, too close for comfort.

He threw the pouch into the helicopter and dived in with the bag. He turned quickly to get the door shut, but he was running out of time before the other man caught him. Andy hurriedly threw the flight bag at the pursuer before he reached the helicopter. Startled, the man reacted as anyone would when being thrown something; he instinctively caught it. As Andy reached up to slide the door shut his right foot caught the black pouch and flicked it out of the open door.

Andy stuck his head out and looked down as the helicopter lifted off. He could see the pouch lying on the ground and the face of the man looking up, still clutching the bag, his tie and raincoat flapping about in the down wash of the helicopter.

"I kicked the diamonds out of the door, Steve," said Andy.

"We have to get out of here," he replied. "That was a tad too close. This place is going to be crawling with police soon." Steve tilted the nose of the Bolkow across the loch and rapidly picked up speed, before rolling into a ninety degree bank to the right, heading back the way they had come only minutes before.

CHAPTER FORTY-TWO
20th June 1990, Cluanie Inn, Scottish Highlands

Mac stared at the rapidly disappearing helicopter for a moment. He had been so close to grabbing the fake police officer. He hurried back to the Inn where a group of four men stood by the entrance, still transfixed by what had taken place.

He spoke to Harris who was now out of the car and staring down the valley at the helicopter.

"Brian, we need to get a lookout broadcast. We need to know where they're going with that."

"Wish we could, Mac. The radios are still out," he said, never taking his eyes off the helicopter.

Mac sighed and shook his head.

Harris turned to the two constables. "MacBrayne, get in touch with Inverness and get them to put a call out to the stations. Anyone not out on patrol needs to get their arse strapped to a car and looking for that chopper. Get Fort William to set up a roadblock on the A87. Use the hotel phone. Keep trying the radio too. Collins, you start collecting statements from that lot." He jerked a thumb towards the assembled crowd trying to see what all the excitement was about.

A second patrol car stopped behind the other marked car. As the officers got out, Harris yelled to them to head back towards Invermoriston and set up a roadblock at the start of the single track section of road.

"Take the details of everyone passing through going south. We're on the lookout for two men travelling together. If anyone can't or won't show ID, arrest them for obstruction or anything else you can conjure up. I don't want these two getting away."

The car spun round in the car park with siren blaring. He turned back to Mac, shaking his head.

"Bloody Bodie and Doyle those two," he muttered.

They were approached by a tall man wearing glasses.

"Are you responding to the robbery call?" he asked.

"What robbery call?" Mac asked.

"We were told the police had called to say there was going to be a robbery."

Harris and Mac exchanged looks.

"Okay, Gentlemen. I'm DCI Harris, Northern Constabulary, and this is DCI MacIntyre, Grampian Police. We need to have a little chat to get to the bottom of this. Shall we go inside?" His tone left no doubt this was not a request.

Inside, Mac addressed the startled young woman at the reception desk. "Is there anywhere we could go to talk to these people in private?"

She nodded towards a door across from the reception desk. "You can use the lounge through there. I'll make sure no one disturbs you."

Mac took out his notebook, "Thank you, Miss...err?"

"MacInnes, Rachel MacInnes."

"Is that a Mc or a Mac?" asked Mac writing in his notebook.

"Mac."

Mac smiled.

"Thank you, Rachel. I'm DCI MacIntyre. Would you mind if I asked you a few questions once we've finished here?"

"I'm not sure I can tell you much. I don't really know what happened, but yes, I'm here until six. Would you like any drinks bringing through?"

Mac shook his head. "Perhaps a bit later."

"Okay, let me know." She reached to answer the telephone which had been ringing throughout their conversation.

Mac smiled and headed into the lounge area where DCI Harris had taken the four.

"Are you going to keep us here long?" asked one of them. "My colleague and I have a flight booked to London this evening."

Harris looked at the man who had spoken. He didn't need to be a detective to deduce these two were unlikely to be local. Not many black folk moved to the Highlands.

"What time?" asked Harris.

"Seventeen-thirty."

Mac noted he had used a twenty-four hour clock format. He wondered if he was military. In fact he wondered if they both were. They certainly had that look about them.

"That depends Mr err...?"

"Silva."

"We'll do our best to get you on your flight, but we do need to find out what happened here and your involvement." He turned to Mac. "Will you do me the honour of having a word with those two over there while I deal with these two?" He nodded towards the other two men.

Mac waved a hand towards the chairs in the opposite corner of the lounge.

"Take a seat please, gentlemen. Right. Where shall we start? Ah yes, your names will do for starters, please."

"Harry Hart."

Mac started to make notes.

"Lenny."

"Just Lenny?"

"Morvern," was added, grudgingly.

"Right. Thank you. That wasn't too difficult was it Mr Morvern? We'll start with you Mr Hart. What exactly was going on here?"

"I'm a diamond dealer as is my associate here. The gentleman over there has some rough diamonds to sell and we were interested in buying them."

Mac seriously doubted Morvern was a diamond dealer. He looked more like a bouncer. A rough diamond dealer. Mac chuckled inside at his own joke.

"You were doing a diamond deal, here?"

Harry nodded. "Yes."

"Why on earth would you do it here?"

Harry pursed his lips and shrugged his shoulders. "Why not? It's a beautiful location."

"And where do you normally trade?"

"London."

"So I reiterate, why here, Mr Hart?"

"Because here is out of the way and none of the other dealers can get a sniff."

"Is that important?"

"Look, Detective, diamonds are a cut-throat business. Always someone trying to muscle in on the deal, undercut you. Sometimes you have to keep it quiet and out of the way. It didn't work though did it?" said Harry.

"Meaning?" asked Mac, slightly puzzled.

"Meaning, someone heard about it didn't they? I'm assuming from your actions out there the helicopter wasn't yours."

Mac ignored the question. "Do you..."

"I don't think we've broken any laws here detective," interrupted the other man.

"That I can't say for sure, Mr ... err...Morvern, but if I find out I will be sure to let you know," said Mac.

"Cheers," said Morvern with a sarcastic sneer.

"Of course you could always admit to something now if you wish. Saves so much time and effort for me."

Lenny shifted uncomfortably in his chair under Mac's gaze. Mac's instincts were telling him there was more to this man than met the eye.

"I think this time Mr Morvern is correct," said Harry. "Diamond deals are done every day, some with cash and some with bank transfers. This happened to be a cash transaction in a remote location."

"And helicopters drop in on these every day?" asked Mac.

"No. I have to say that's a first."

"Is it only the two of you making this purchase?"

"Yes, although technically speaking Mr Morvern is...well I suppose you could say he is the bag man, he is carrying the money."

"Is that what's in the black case?"

"Yes."

"How much?"

"One million in cash, another two million in bearer bonds."

Mac almost choked. "You are casually walking around with three million pounds in a case?"

"Dollars, detective, and we often send valuable diamonds through the post. Why would anyone suspect the contents? Out in the open is often the safest place to hide something. If the case was handcuffed to the carrier it would signal to the world it had a value. By doing it this way, it could be the latest report on the numbers of great crested newts in the case as far as anyone knows."

Mac ran his hand through his hair. "Assuming this is all above board, who knows about it?"

"Just us."

"The four of you in this room?"

"Yes."

"So tell me how do you think this helicopter became involved?"

"One of your lot called the Inn and said you'd heard there was going to be an attempted robbery and that a helicopter was coming to take the diamonds and the money into safe-keeping until you could get some officers here."

"You had a call from the police?"

"Yes."

"And who took this call?"

"The girl at the reception desk. She came in here and said she'd had a phone call from the police. She asked if we knew anything about some diamonds. She then told us what I just told you."

"And then what?"

"We asked if we could call someone to verify the story."

"Did you?"

"She gave us the name and number she had been given, so I rang it."

"Who answered?"

"Northern Constabulary, at least that's what they said. I asked to speak to the name I'd been given and I was put through."

"Can you remember the name?"

Harry nodded towards DCI Harris. "It was him. I was surprised when he said his name. I couldn't see how he could get here from Inverness in that short time. Look, detective, what's going on here?"

Mac sighed, "Mr Hart, if I knew I would be a lot happier."

CHAPTER FORTY-THREE
20th June 1990, Loch Cluanie, Scottish Highlands

"Northern Constabulary. How may I help you?"

The line was crackly and the officer had to repeat himself several times as he gave his details and asked to speak to the duty inspector.

"One moment please, I'll put you through."

He smiled at the young lady on reception. "Nice day for it, whatever it is that happened."

She returned the smile. "I was hoping someone could tell me."

"Ach I'll be the last to know."

"Inspector Young," a voice announced in the handset.

The officer put up his hand and smiled to cut off the receptionist's reply.

"He must be new," the policeman thought. He didn't recognise the voice or the name. Another Inspector to break in. That was all he needed.

It took a few minutes to relate the events to the inspector, and relay DCI Harris' roadblock instructions. He had to repeat several times that all officers should be on a look out for a police helicopter, before the Inspector understood.

"We'll do our best but let DCI Harris know we still have no operational radios, and no contact with Kyle by phone either. I'll get hold of Fort William and we'll see what we can get organised. If this line is anything to go by, we might be better sending pigeons."

On the top of a telegraph pole at the dam end of Loch Cluanie, Roddy slipped his headset off one ear and started to roll a cigarette. He was getting quite good at playing policemen. Maybe he should take up acting for a career.

As he lit up, he thought about the money that coming his way soon. Cut off the phones, install the box and intercept some calls, that was his part. Oh, and make a radio call when the *Polis* went tearing past him. He didn't know all the details, which was part of the arrangement. Though now he knew it really did involve a helicopter. Next stop Ceannacroc and take the VHF repeater out of the telephone call box. Not exactly busy for his last day of work.

CHAPTER FORTY-FOUR

20th June 1990, Glen Shiel, Scottish Highlands

Steve kept the Bolkow two hundred and fifty feet above the main road heading back down the valley. The road was busy with cars heading to and from the Kyle of Lochalsh. If the police interviewed any of these drivers, the direction they were flying would suggest an escape to the West.

Once again Andy was navigating.

"The next valley to the right is the one we want, appears to be a dead end, well it is really, but once we drop over the ridge we can head back towards the landing site."

Steve already knew this, having gone over the route so many times on the OS maps and the two of them had scouted out several of the valleys on their dirt bikes. It was all well and good looking at a map but nothing could beat being there in person and seeing it for yourself. The adrenalin was still pumping and Steve was fighting to stay calm. That had been close, and closer still for Andy. No wonder he was gabbling on a bit.

"Okay, Andy. Got the valley in sight. You best make sure you are strapped in, mate. Some of these turns will be a little tight."

"Oh I'm strapped in all right," Andy laughed. "I know all about your flying already remember."

Steve lifted the collective lever a touch as they turned right into the valley.

At the top they would almost be visible from the Inn, so Steve held the helicopter low; the skids skimming the heather as they crested the ridge. From here he could see directly into Glen Affric. He dropped down the other side, increasing speed rapidly. They had to get back to the Land Rover as quickly as possible and Steve was pushing the helicopter to the limit, not to mention his own abilities. In less than two minutes they were in the Glen, and Steve rolled the Bolkow hard to the right, the blades making a clattering sound from the effort of keeping the machine in the air.

"Jeez, Steve, take it easy mate."

"Don't worry. If we crash, I get to the scene of the accident first, and I've no intention of arriving there at all."

"I'm more concerned about the contents of my stomach right now."

"That'll be the adrenaline mate."

"If you say so."

It was five more minutes to the next turn, giving Steve a chance to scan the instruments. As he did, he frowned. The fuel pressure on number two engine was dropping. He reached up and switched off the fuel boost pump, then switched it on again. The pressure continued to drop.

Andy saw him operate the switch for a second time.

"Something you want to tell me?"

"Looks like we lost number two fuel boost pump."

"And that means?"

"That means trouble. Normally it wouldn't, because the engine-driven mechanical pump can supply enough fuel to the engine. Unfortunately there's not a lot in the tanks so it will draw air. I was a passenger on a fishery protection flight and saw it happen."

"As you're talking to me now, I assume the outcome was good."

"Aye, the outcome was good, but we'll effectively be single engine. It'll start popping and I'll have to throttle back."

"We can still fly though can't we?"

"Aye, flying isn't the problem. Landing is. We'll probably over torque the good engine if we try to go into the hover."

"I'm assuming we can't get out and leave the helicopter up here, so what do we do to land?"

"We have to land like an aeroplane, with forward speed, so the airflow over the blades is doing some of the work."

"Land like an aeroplane?" Andy asked. "I hate to be the one to point this out mate, but we don't have any wheels, just two scaffolding poles welded to the bottom."

Steve laughed. "I thought you might notice that. We have to slide the skids along the ground. A run-on landing."

"We're not going back to the landing site then are we?"

"We'll head that way, but I think we'll lose the engine before we get there. It's too rough in the clearing and way too short for a run-on. We need to be doing about forty knots at touch down."

"Bugger."

"Exactly."

"So where are we going if we need to do this run-on?"

"The only place is the road. But let's hope it doesn't come to that and we can land at the site."

"And if there are cars on the road?"

"We can make one pass but no more. After that we're landing, cars or not."

"Terrific!"

They continued on course for a couple of minutes until almost at the end of Loch Affric. Steve turned the helicopter to the right, into a small valley. They were not far from the landing site now. There was still a slight chance they would make it. As the thought entered Steve's head, the number two engine popped and spluttered.

"Right on cue," he mused as he reached up and retarded the power lever to idle.

"Looks like the decision is made," he announced. "There's a straight section of road after the power lines, just to the east of the village. That's where we'll land. The Land Rover is part way down it. If I land on the Cluanie side of the Land Rover we can block the road to anyone coming from the Inn."

"You already knew it would be suitable for a landing, didn't you?"

"Aye, because I checked it out when I was doing the planning."

"Now why doesn't that surprise me?"

"Got to look for alternatives, always. It's a bit tight with the trees around, but it should be wide enough."

"Steve, are you happy doing this? Is there nowhere else we could go?"

"We don't have enough fuel to go anywhere else. In any case, how would we get away?"

"We wouldn't, but we'd be alive."

"Ach we'll live. Be a doddle. It means they'll find the helicopter a bit sooner. Be a bit obvious sat in the middle of the road."

They lapsed into silence as Steve altered course towards the road.

Andy broke the silence.

"Just a thought mate. You have done this sort of landing before haven't you?"

The long pause gave Andy the answer even before Steve shook his head and said, "Nope."

CHAPTER FORTY-FIVE
20th June 1990, Cluanie Inn, Scottish Highlands

Well, that was interesting, thought Nicky. He had just witnessed some strange happenings. Lenny and the man he couldn't quite place, plus two people who were clearly foreigners, were mixed up in something. The odd thing was, he had seen Mac chase another officer towards a police helicopter, which had left the scene rapidly. You didn't have to be a journalist to know there was a story in this. Trouble was he couldn't go inside to find out what it was. He still had to stay out of Lenny's sight. He didn't want to tip his hand. No, he would have to sit it out, then try to collar Mac as he left.

Whilst he waited, another policeman asked him to give a statement about what he had seen. Nicky said he hadn't seen anything, he'd arrived after it had all happened and stopped to see what the fuss was about.

It was another two hours before he saw the four men leave, in two separate cars. Whatever it was they were up to, they clearly had met here, not travelled together. Twenty minutes later he was rewarded with the sight of Mac and another person leaving the Inn.

He got out of his car and dashed across the road.

"DCI MacIntyre," he shouted.

Mac turned to find the source of the shout.

"Rolands. What the hell are you doing here?" He turned to the other man with him. "Brian, meet Nicky Rolands. One of the leeches working for the P and J."

"Aww that's a little unfair, detective. I'm only doing my job."

"Aye, so we keep hearing. What are you doing here anyway?"

"I was going to ask you the same question."

"Listen, sonny, I ask the questions, you do the answering. That's how policing works."

Nicky thought for a moment. "What if I can give you some information, would you give me an exclusive?"

"If you have information about a crime and you withhold it, what I will give you is a cell."

"Perhaps we should hear what he has to say," said DCI Harris.

Mac grunted. "Right, back to the Inn. This better be good, Rolands, or you're going to get a ride in a squad car."

"So you're telling me this Morvern character is muscle for a London villain by the name of Munro?"

"I don't know if he is now, but last I heard he was. He went off the rails a bit when his father committed suicide. Turned to crime apparently. Least that's what I heard one time when I was home."

"And when was that?" asked Mac.

"Ten, twelve years ago maybe."

"What do you know about this Munro character then?"

"Nasty piece of work, detective. He's proper gangland he is. Old school. Came from Glasgow in the sixties. Usual, drugs, gambling, prostitution. You name it he does it. Runs a diamond business too. That's supposed to be legit but there are rumours. The East End is his patch. No one crosses Munro."

Mac looked at Harris. "Are you thinking what I'm thinking?"

"I think I'm thinking what you're thinking."

"Are you going to tell me what this is about?" asked Nicky.

"What else do you know?" asked Mac.

"Are you going to let me in on what happened?"

Mac thought for a moment, "What did Morvern's father do for a living?"

"I dunno. Most people round there worked in the docks. I don't think Lenny's dad did though. You know, something in the back of my mind tells me he was a jeweller or something. What's this all about?"

The two detectives exchanged glances again.

"One word of this gets out before I give you the go ahead, Rolands, and your feet won't touch the ground. Do I make myself clear?"

Nicky nodded. Finally this could be the break he was looking for. Fleet Street here I come.

CHAPTER FORTY-SIX

20th June 1990, Glen Moriston, Scottish Highlands

The fuel pressure on number two engine steadfastly refused to rise, despite Steve's repeated attempts with the switch.

"Please tell me you're joking. You practised this in the sim, right?"

Steve shook his head.

"Sorry mate, it's no joke. This will be the first time. So you best get buckled up tight."

Glen Moriston is a wide shallow glen, along which flows the River Moriston. The river shares the valley with the A887, which crosses the river twice on its journey to Invermoriston. The valley floor is a mixture of farming and forestry, which stretches to the lower slopes of the hills before giving way to heather and ultimately the rocky crags of Carn a' Chaocain to the North and Meall Dubh to the South.

Steve flew over the river, parallel to the road. The helicopter would be visible from the main road, but as long as they got into the Land Rover unseen it would be ok. This section of road wasn't particularly busy; most of the tourists avoided the single-track road beyond, and elected to come via Invergarry and the A87, but it would only need one witness to jeopardise their escape plan.

"Looks clear both ways so let's get on the ground while we can. We've only got one shot at this".

Steve pulled up the nose of the Bolkow and made a tight turn to bring the helicopter round 180 degrees, facing back the way they had come. The manoeuvre reduced his airspeed sufficiently for the approach. He aimed to touchdown a few yards before the forest road where they left the Land Rover. He kept the speed at 45 knots and gently lowered the collective lever so the aircraft descended towards the road. Even at this relatively low speed the trees seemed to rush by the sides of the helicopter.

As the skids contacted the road he lowered the collective lever fully, but kept a small amount of backward pressure on the cyclic stick, keeping the weight of the helicopter off the front of the skids, reducing the chance of the helicopter tipping over on its nose. The noise of the skids on the tarmac was a gentle hiss, and the landing much smoother than he expected. Steve used the yaw pedals to keep the helicopter straight as the speed dropped away.

"You sure you've not done that before, kiddo?" asked Andy with a nervous chuckle. "Seemed pretty good to me."

"Beginner's luck, mate. Hold on, got one more trick up my sleeve."

Steve pulled up on the collective to make the Bolkow light on its skids again and applied right pedal pressure causing the helicopter to slew round in the road. Once it was at ninety degrees to the carriageway he lowered the collective and started the shutdown procedure. He couldn't waste time allowing the engines to cool before shutting them down. They needed to move fast. He turned off the fuel and switched off the battery.

"We better get going before someone turns up to find out what's happening," he yelled. "Grab everything and go."

They jumped out with the blades still turning and collected items from inside the cabin and the boot. Steve took a final look, making sure nothing incriminating remained.

The helicopter tail rested over the small bushes at the road edge, the nose close to the barrier on the opposite side. It would be almost impossible to squeeze a vehicle past.

Satisfied they had everything, they jogged down the road towards Invermoriston. They were fifty yards from the forest road entrance. Andy dropped the things he was carrying and opened the gate. Steve carried on through to the Land Rover closely followed by his pal. Between them they removed the camouflage net and stashed the items in the back of the vehicle. They removed their flight gear, and each got into a pair of Forestry Commission overalls, tossing the flight gear in with the rest of the equipment and items removed from the helicopter. Steve threw a small tarpaulin over the top and Andy pulled the generator and pressure washer in front of the pile, laying a petrol strimmer and chainsaw on top. A cursory glance would suggest they were genuine forestry workers. Not that Steve expected to be stopped. The radios would still be useless and setting up any form of road block would be a difficult task for the police to co-ordinate without them. And now, with the helicopter blocking the road, there were bigger problems; a twenty-five mile detour for anyone who wanted to get to Invermoriston. Unless a police car was already ahead of them, they would be well away before the police could respond.

Steve drove the Land Rover out of the forest and Andy shut the gate behind them, placing the sawn-through padlock back in its place. It would be some time before anyone discovered the damage.

Andy leapt back in the Land Rover and they set off.

"That didn't go quite to plan," he said.

"You can say that again. I've had enough excitement today to last me for a while. Do you think they got a good enough look to identify us?"

"I doubt it, not with the helmets and sunglasses. Sure, they'll know my height and size but not much more. They wouldn't be able to see into the chopper at all."

"Now all we need to do is keep to our story, I'm sure we'll be questioned, but as long as we stick to the story, they can't prove a thing."

"I feel knackered," Andy said. "I think the adrenaline has worn off."

"I know what you mean, mate."

As they reached the end of the straight, a police car came around the corner at the opposite end, in time to spot the tail end of the Land Rover disappearing in the distance.

CHAPTER FORTY-SEVEN

20th June 1990, Ceannacroc, Scottish Highlands

"What the f...?"

The two officers despatched in the marked car towards Invermoriston, stared out of the windscreen. They were supposed to be setting up a roadblock. A roadblock appeared to have been set up already, in the form of a helicopter across the carriageway.

"Just a hunch, mate, but this might be the one we are looking for."

"You think? You don't think Strathclyde have just parked here and gone for a wee wander in the hills?"

"Aye mebbe, but probably not."

They both laughed.

"I wonder why they landed here, it isn't exactly hidden is it?"

"Nah. You'd think dropping it in the forest somewhere would be better. Could stay hidden for weeks."

The officers could see the scrape marks along the road where the skids had slid along. There was no other damage to the road surface, only scrape marks. Clearly the helicopter had turned at the last moment as it was parked ninety degrees to the marks.

"We'll have to go back to Ceannacroc and phone it in. See if we can get a roadblock set up at Invermoriston. How they're going to get the message out through this noise I've no idea."

CHAPTER FORTY-EIGHT
20th June 1990, Scottish Highlands

"Shit."

"What? What's happened?" Andy asked.

"I just caught a glimpse of a car in the mirror as we came around the corner."

"Damn."

"It gets worse, it's a police car. If they saw us they know we have a Land Rover now. I just hope they can't squeeze past. I don't think they can."

"This isn't exactly a brilliant getaway vehicle is it?" laughed Andy.

"It would've been if we hadn't had to do that landing. Blends right in. Not built for speed though, I agree."

"Not built for comfort either."

"There's a long straight coming up. We'll soon know if they got through. If they aren't in sight we'll pull over somewhere and get this Forestry Commission signage off. That might throw them off the trail at least, that's if they even saw us."

On the next long straight, Steve kept his eyes glued to the mirror.

"Looks like they didn't get through. We'll stop at the next lay-by, get the signs off and bury some of this other stuff if we can."

Twenty minutes later Andy put a spade into the back of the Land Rover.

"That lot should stay hidden for a while," he said.

The flight suits, Decca map roll and various other items from the helicopter, along with the Forestry Commission signs and overalls were buried in the top of the river bank. What remained in the back of the Land Rover could be explained away if stopped. Now they were two guys returning from a week away fishing, albeit with some rather strange items on board.

The rest of the journey to Invermoriston passed uneventfully, passing only a handful of cars until they were close to the village.

Steve pulled into the car park of the Glenmoriston Hotel and dashed across the road to the Post Office. He returned a few minutes later with two steaming cartons of coffee and two bacon rolls.

"I think we deserve these."

A police car from Inverness swung in from the main road and pulled across the road behind them as they left the car park. Exiting from the Hotel, they had been ignored.

The pair looked at each other and burst out laughing.

"It's all about timing," quipped Andy.

CHAPTER FORTY-NINE
20th June 1990, Central London

The police appeared satisfied with the answers from Ollie and Pereira, and although technically the diamonds were imported illegally, they were only concerned with the attempted robbery and the theft of the helicopter. The police allowed the pair to leave the Cluanie Inn and catch the last Dan-Air flight back to London. It was a close thing; they arrived at the airport thirty minutes before departure.

When they reached the hotel in central London, Ollie told Pereira he needed time to consider their next move. It would be best if they went to their own rooms and settled down for the night. Ollie would let the Lieutenant know what he had decided over breakfast.

Pereira was about to object when Ollie said,

"It's been a most difficult day. I'm sure things will look a lot better in the morning when I've had a chance to re-assess the situation. I'm tired."

Pereira took the hint and headed off to his room with the diamonds. Ollie said he would go to the bar for a small nightcap first and made off in that direction. He glanced over his shoulder to watch as the Lieutenant got into the lift then doubled back to the reception desk.

"I believe there may be a package here for me?"

"Yes, Sir. We were instructed not to give it to you when you checked in if you were accompanied."

The receptionist handed over small parcel. Ollie thanked her and headed up to his room to inspect the contents.

CHAPTER FIFTY
21st June 1990, Central London

Pereira tried Ollie's room once more; no reply. As the morning progressed, the Lieutenant's concern increased. He had not seen the Major since the night before and he wasn't at breakfast. Although he was anxious, the Major had said he needed time to re-assess the situation. Perhaps the Major was somewhere in the city trying to arrange another deal. After all, the diamonds were still with Pereira. It wasn't likely the Major would run off without them.

Pereira had a moment of panic. What if the diamonds weren't there? He went to the case lying on the dresser. He unlocked it and pulled out the black bag, emptying the contents carefully onto the surface of the dresser.

They looked like the stones he had seen before. It was hard to imagine these pieces of rock were valuable, and that is all they were, pieces of rock. He telephoned the Major's room once more and still got no answer.

Two hours later, he plucked up courage to knock on the Major's door. There was no response. He could leave it no longer. He went to the reception desk and told them of his concerns. His friend had been unwell the night before. He should have heard something from him by now. He asked if someone could go to the room and check on his welfare.

The duty manager reluctantly agreed and Pereira accompanied him.

Once inside the room, it was clear the bed had not been slept in. All the Major's clothes were still in the closet, his suitcase was there and his passport lay on the bedside cabinet. If the Major had gone somewhere, it wasn't far.

"Your friend appears not to have slept here."

"So I see. Perhaps he was feeling better and went hunting."

"Hunting?"

"Yes. Ladies. You know?"

"Ah I see. So you don't wish me to contact the police and report him missing?"

The last thing Pereira wanted was the police to be involved.

"No. He will turn up. I only wanted to make sure he was not ill in his room. Thank you."

Back in his room Pereira ran through everything in his mind again. He had gone through the Major's file before meeting him in the General's office. There was nothing there to suggest he was anything other than a soldier loyal to the UNITA cause. He had only joined after his father had been killed, but many soldiers needed a turning point in their lives to take up arms. That had been the trigger for the Major.

Despite the lack of anything significant in the Major's file, Pereira still could not shake off the unease he had felt back in Angola. Now it appeared to be justified.

Pereira wondered if the absence was any way related to the men they met yesterday. The tall, dark-haired one was clearly the brains. He knew diamonds well. He suspected the other man was a bodyguard. Perhaps they had been in touch and the Major was indeed in another meeting. Why had he not seen fit to tell Pereira?

He decided to wait two more hours before sending a message to the General. The message would take time to get to Angola but at least he would have covered himself before returning without the Major. The flight to Lusaka was not until Saturday so there was time for the Major to return. After that, he was on his own. Pereira had his orders and he would abide by them.

CHAPTER FIFTY-ONE
21st June 1990, Wapping, London

"What the hell happened, Lenny? I give you one simple task. 'Look after the money,' I said. 'Yes, Mr Munro,' you said. And what happens? I'll tell you what happens, you cretin. You come back with four thousand dollars. Four thousand! I send you with one million in cash and you come back with just four thousand. And to top it off, you lose another two million in bearer bonds too. This story better be good, Lenny. You can bet your life on that."

Lenny had been told to sit in the reception area of Munro's office, otherwise he would be towering over his boss, and that would take away some intimidation Donald was trying to bring to bear on him. He wasn't entirely sure if Lenny had been completely stupid or very clever. The simple fact was Donald was down by almost two and a half million dollars, in cash and bearer bonds. He was sure Harry Hart was behind this somehow, but how he couldn't figure out yet. How had he managed to make a switch? Unless Lenny was being economical with the truth of course. He didn't think Lenny had the mental capacity to pull off a con like this, but who knows what Hart had promised him. On the other hand, if Lenny was involved why did he come back knowing Donald was going to be unhappy he had lost two and a half million dollars? Donald's head was beginning to spin with trying to make sense of the situation. Lenny couldn't have known, could he?

"I'm telling you, Mr Munro the case never left my sight apart from when the rozzer took it."

"Yes, Lenny. Tell me again about the flying pigs."

A look of puzzlement crossed Lenny's face for a moment, then Donald saw the penny drop in Lenny's eyes.

"Oh, the helicopter, Mr Munro."

"Jesus wept Lenny. Yes, of course I mean the helicopter."

Donald shook his head. If Lenny was involved in this, then he should win every Oscar, BAFTA and any other acting award from now until the day he dies. The man was simply too stupid to pull off a stunt like this.

"Well, it was mainly white...."

"Lenny, you moron!" screamed Donald. "I don't want a description of the helicopter, I want you to tell me what happened."

"Oh. Right. Well, like I said before, Mr Munro, we were in the lounge where Mr Hart and the other geezer were looking at the diamonds, when the bird from reception came in and said the police had phoned to say there was going to be some sort of hit on us. Mr Hart went and phoned them to check it out. Sure enough the geezer on the other end of the phone confirmed it."

"Are you sure it was the police, Lenny, not some sort of con?"

Lenny beamed a smile. "I sure am Mr Munro, cos I checked the number in the phone book after."

He looked really pleased with himself and Donald was taken aback slightly. Lenny had done something on his own initiative.

"Carry on, Lenny."

"Well, they told Mr Hart a helicopter was coming to remove the diamonds and the cash, and police cars were coming to try to catch the bad guys."

"And did no one think to ask why they were going to take the diamonds and the cash, or even how they knew about them?"

Lenny frowned.

"No one thought of that, Mr Munro. It seemed reasonable at the time."

"It would Lenny, that's how a con works," he said shaking his head. "Carry on."

"This police chopper turns up and a guy comes over to us and has a chat with Mr Hart. I have to say he didn't seem to be too happy handing the stuff over. Anyways, he does and the guy starts going back to the chopper. Just then the some more rozzers turn up and one of them starts to run after the guy. He legs it to the chopper and dives in. He sees the rozzer is about to catch him, so he chucks the case at him. I don't know exactly what happened then, but I saw the bag with the diamonds in fall out of the chopper as they took off. I swear Mr Munro, apart from that moment the case wasn't out of my sight."

"Could anyone have been in your room, Lenny? You know, while you were in the bar or something."

Lenny beamed again. "I would've known. I put a hair across the door. I learnt that from a James Bond film. It was still there when I went back."

Donald looked at Lenny.

"Lenny, son, I must be getting soft in my old age. I believe you. That, and the fact I don't think you have enough brain cells to pull one over on me. But we are going to get to the bottom of this. Someone has the money and I intend to find out who, and not even heaven will be able to help them when I do. Now get out my sight before I change my mind."

Lenny for once was quick on the uptake and dashed out of the door as fast as he could. Once he had gone, Eddie spoke.

"Boss? You're not going to let him get away with it, are you?"

Donald looked at him with his head on one side, his Glaswegian accent taking on a life of its own.

"Do ye really think I'm going saft in the heid, Eddie? Of course I'm no letting him get away with it. But at the moment he's the only one who can lead us to the money, or the diamonds, or mebbe both. Whatever is going on, Lenny is the key to it, I'm sure. Once a ha' ma money back I don't want to see his face around here again. Am I clear on that Eddie?"

Eddie nodded frantically.

"Yes, boss. Crystal."

"So in the meantime, you and the boys are going to stick to him like the proverbial on the blanket. I don't want you to let him out of your sight, but, I don't want him to know you're there either."

Donald waited a moment.

"Why are you still here?"

Eddie left in a hurry. The boss was not a man to be around when he was angry, and losing two and a half million made him very angry.

CHAPTER FIFTY-TWO
22nd June 1990, Peterhead, Aberdeenshire

The incident room in Peterhead police station was crowded again. Not only were detectives working on the stolen helicopter case, but there were also some of the Northern Constabulary officers who were now involved in the attempted diamond robbery.

Mac and Harris chatted together at the front of the room whilst the rest of the officers sorted themselves out so everyone could sit.

Amid scraping of chairs and ribald comments, the two forces settled down. The air buzzed as rumours of the robbery attempt filtered through the room.

Mac stood and waited for the noise to die down before he spoke.

"Right you lot, pay attention. Some of you will be aware of what happened and some of you won't, so I'll start at the beginning. Yesterday, as part of the follow-up to the helicopter theft, I was in Inverness liaising with DCI Harris here, who some of you will already know. While there, a call came in to say there was a helicopter near the Cluanie Inn on Loch Cluanie. For those of you who are geographically challenged..." Mac paused and looked at DC Halliday,

"Robbie..."

A roar of laughter came from the Peterhead officers. Robbie had once spent half an hour trying to locate an address in Strichen, to interview a witness, when he should have been fifty miles away in Strachen.

"... Loch Cluanie is on the A87 which is the main road to Kyle of Lochalsh." Mac continued with the briefing, filling in the officers on the events of the previous day.

"So now we know where and why, but we don't know who. We do however know the whereabouts of the helicopter. Whether it was for a quick getaway, or some other reason, we aren't sure, but the thieves abandoned the helicopter on the A887, completely blocking the road. Bond are sending up a team to recover it now SOCO have finished with it. At least we know where it is, and why it was stolen. Our job now is to try to find out who. Some of you will have noticed we have some colleagues from Northern with us today. That's because this is now a combined operation. The original theft is ours, and the attempted robbery is theirs, but as we are assuming both these actions were carried out by the same people, we are now pooling our resources."

"Will they get all the glory, Sir?" asked DC Leask.

This brought a few catcalls from the Northern officers.

"Probably, Jimmy. You know how it is with these rural forces," Mac said laughing. "Okay. We know at least two people are involved, because we saw them. One is Caucasian, approximately 5"10", stocky build but not fat, clean shaven. Other than that, I can't give a better description, as he was wearing a helmet with a dark visor. None of the people interviewed at the scene could give any better description, other than he spoke with an English accent. The second person, flying the helicopter, is also Caucasian, I think. I was getting blown about at that point, so it was hard to see."

One of the Northern officers spoke up. "Do we have any leads on possibles, Sir?

"We have a Bond employee unaccounted for at the moment. An engineer, Stephen Hayling. He's away on a fishing trip with another engineer," Mac paused whilst he consulted his notes, "one Andrew Mannion, who is employed on the flight simulator at Aberdeen. It would appear both have had time flying in the simulator, something the employers were aware of, and turned a blind eye to. At the moment we have no idea whether either of them is capable of flying a helicopter for real. All I can say is, from the way it flew off, I would be surprised to find out it wasn't a professional pilot doing the flying. We believe there are more than two people involved and they may well be from outside the local area. Our enquiries would lead us to believe the theft of the helicopter was carried out by someone who knew about the security and layout of Longside. It may well be this engineer and his mate are implicated. Hayling is due back on shift on Saturday, and Mannion back at work on Monday. We'll be having a wee chat with them as soon as they return."

Mac turned to DCI Harris, "Anything you want to add?"

Harris got up from his chair and addressed the room.

"The operation from our point of view is to apprehend the persons responsible for an attempted theft of approximately six million dollars' worth of diamonds, and three million dollars in cash and bearer bonds."

Several of the officers let out quiet whistles of surprise. Harris nodded.

"Apparently, these sorts of deals are not uncommon, although they are not usually carried out in the Highlands of Scotland. It would appear the location was chosen because one of the dealers knew it from a holiday visit, and wanted to be away from other dealers when the transaction took place. Possible, even plausible, but my instincts tell me there is more to it. One of the men is a known associate of an ex-Glasgow gang member, one Donald Munro, who has been suspected of numerous crimes in London, including murder. Unfortunately, he manages to remain squeaky clean every time, and so far the Met have not been able to pin so much as a parking ticket on him. He's a gemstone dealer. How legitimate remains to be seen. The fact he's involved does make it seem more likely this wasn't a kosher deal, however the other buyer is a reputable dealer, and as far as we know, he's snow-white. All parties concerned were allowed on their way after questioning. There was a possibility of a breach of VAT regulations but it would be hard to prove there was an intention to avoid VAT, as no deal had actually taken place. We'll let HM Customs worry about that one. We have bigger fish to catch."

He continued. "We also know communications were compromised deliberately. Constable MacBrayne who put the call through to Northern HQ, mentioned to me he didn't recognise the Inspector he spoke to. He was right to do so, as HQ never received the call. Enquiries are still ongoing for that and for the radio interference which ceased four hours after the robbery attempt, and has not recurred. If anyone has any ideas you can speak to myself or DCI MacIntyre. If we are not available then either DI Kerr or DS Grant will be here at Peterhead, along with DS Halliwell who will remain here as liaison officer, once we go back to God's own country."

That brought a few catcalls from the Peterhead officers and a few "Hard lucks" from the Northern officers.

"Clearly we have a lot of work to do with multiple lines of enquiries, so the sooner we get onto it the better."

CHAPTER FIFTY-THREE
25th June 1990, Peterhead, Aberdeenshire

The investigation team for the helicopter theft was swamped with a pile of reports and information. Few sightings were reported prior to the robbery attempt, but since the release of that news, things had changed dramatically, with a deluge of reported sightings. Each report had to be investigated thoroughly. Most were normal air traffic, but one might just lead to the thieves.

Was it any wonder investigating crimes was such a laborious process, Mac thought. Some of the statements taken from eyewitnesses defied belief. One person was adamant it involved an RAF Search and Rescue machine, while another saw at least four men in the helicopter. Obviously, the team discounted any reports which were clearly at odds with what the Police Officers saw, but some of the others had to be investigated, no matter how bizarre.

Mac approached DS Grant.

"How's the forensics going, Alan?"

"We've got tyre marks up at the barn, boot prints as well, but not much more than that. The helicopter was clearly there. Traces of oil in the barn and scrape marks where it was pushed in and out, and there were tracks from those wheels they attach to the skids."

"Any word on the fake phone calls?"

He handed Mac a report sheet.

"Clever buggers aren't they?" Mac grunted. "Exchange lines rerouted. This missing BT engineer..." Mac looked at the report again, "...Johnstone, think there's any link with Hayling or Mannion? Has he disappeared voluntarily or has he been made to disappear?"

"If we can find a link between either of them and the BT guy then maybe we can crack the case. And there must be others involved too. Quite apart from the flying side, there must have been a lot of other preparation."

"Linking them to anyone else isn't proving to be easy. We have Hayling's phone records for the past few months. One brief phone call from a callbox in London and several from a callbox in Balmacara, near the campsite, but they stopped in April. I'm thinking he maybe had a girlfriend over there, though come to think of it they stopped a short while after the call from London. With them being callboxes it's a dead end. A couple of calls to Balmacara Campsite and the rest of the calls are local, and not many of them either. If they were planning anything it wasn't by phone. Mannion hasn't had a phone for the past six months. Cut off."

Grant grimaced.

"Get hold of the pilots at Bond and find out about Hayling's flying skills. Maybe he was the one who flew it out. See what they think." Mac said.

Grant leaned back in his chair.

"I think those two are the key to this. If only we could place them at the scene."

"Aye. There are a lot of 'if onlys' in this world Alan. If only I could win the football pools I'd be on a yacht in the Med right now."

"Och we'll get them, Sir. Just have to keep digging and see what we can come up with."

Mac walked over to DS Halliwell from Northern Constabulary who was still acting as liaison between Grampian and Northern forces.

"Good morning Tony, how's it going?"

"Morning, Sir. Well, not too well I'm afraid. We've followed up on the link with this Munro fella. As they didn't do anything wrong I can't see where we can go with it. The Met did say, 'Please tell us you have something on that bastard'."

Mac laughed.

"I take it they've been after him for a while eh?"

"Seems so. He's suspected of several murders, drug and prostitution rackets and any number of crimes they would like to solve."

"From the sounds of it they aren't going to get lucky this time either."

Mac had a thought.

"I wonder if there's any link between Hayling, Mannion and this Munro fella. It could make sense you know. He didn't want to pay for the diamonds, a straightforward robbery would be too obvious, but if a third party were to carry out the robbery...well who would think it was him? Maybe that was what the phone call from London was about. It wasn't a long one but maybe enough to set up a meeting." He sat in thought for a moment perched on the edge of the desk then said,

"What about the jeweller, Hart, anything there?"

Halliwell shook his head.

"Nah. He's whiter than white. Well respected. Files his tax returns early. Everything above board. Makes you wonder how he got involved with this Munro character though."

"Aye, well they are often the ones to watch."

"Strange thing is we can't get hold of him. Met have dropped round to his offices a couple of times but haven't caught him in yet. Seems these diamond dealers often disappear for a wee while, off buying or selling somewhere."

Mac ran his hand over his head.

"Hmm...my instincts are telling me there might be more to it. He's not the first person involved to have disappeared. Strangely enough our two main suspects are still carrying on as normal. Makes me doubt if we're on the right lines. What are we missing here?" He paused. "Anything else I should know?"

"Not unless you want to go and see Mrs MacCafferty in Beauly. She thinks it was aliens she saw that night who tried to steal the diamonds."

Mac roared with laughter.

"Oh no. That pleasure is all yours."

"Thanks, Sir," Halliwell said with a sardonic smile.

CHAPTER FIFTY-FOUR

26th June 1990, Peterhead, Aberdeenshire

DS Grant glanced up from his desk on hearing Mac laugh. It was a long time since he had seen him so relaxed. He wondered what had brought about the change. Surely Mac must be feeling the pressure to get this one solved. Even though it had not turned out to be terrorist related, it was still an embarrassment not to catch the perpetrators. Stealing a helicopter wasn't an everyday event and the press were not letting it go. They wanted answers. Grant was gradually coming around to Mac's way of thinking about the press. If they want answers, go out and find them instead of hassling the officers who were doing their best.

Grant looked through the reports again. He was sure he was missing something, something to tie Hayling and Mannion to at least the theft, if not the attempted robbery.

They knew where the helicopter had been stored but the site had given them little to go on. A check of the campsite at Balmacara had confirmed Hayling had been there, and the pitch had a tent on it for the time he said. Other than that they couldn't say whether he was on site or not. Although they knew him well as he was a frequent visitor, they certainly did not take notice of his movements, nor any of their campers.

No. It was here somewhere, he knew it.

Hayling drove a Land Rover, and a Land Rover had been seen near the abandoned helicopter. Land Rover tyre tracks were at the barn. Hayling and Mannion had been in the area at the time of the attempted robbery. However, they hadn't been near Peterhead at the time of the theft, but it didn't mean they couldn't have been there.

Grant's head was hurting. He needed a break from this. Eighteen straight days they had been working on this case. First trying to find the helicopter, and then trying to find the culprits.

He took his jacket from the chair.

"Going for a bit of air, Sir, fancy a walk?"

Mac pursed his lips.

"Yeah, why not? Bit of sea air might do me some good."

From Peterhead Police Station, they wandered down the road to Bath Street and turned left towards the harbour. Peterhead was still a busy fishing port as well as a major support base for the offshore oil industry. The smell of pickle reached Grant's nose on the unusually calm breeze. The Cross and Blackwell factory at the other end of the road ran several product lines. The residents could always tell when it was Branston Pickle day.

Mac broke the silence first and related his theory about a connection between Hayling, Mannion and Munro.

"You think it's possible, Sir?" asked Grant.

"It would make sense. Munro gets everything and pays for nothing. Even his partner in this seems to have disappeared.

Arrange the robbery then get rid of the crew. No witnesses, no one to turn Queen's evidence."

"If that's the case then Mannion and Hayling could be next."

"Aye, they could well be."

"Good thing we're keeping an eye on them."

They walked on in silence, then Grant asked.

"Are you okay, Sir?"

Mac looked at Grant.

"Aye I'm fine, Alan, why do you ask that?"

"Well...it's just that for a while now you've seemed preoccupied. And today you burst out laughing at something Tony said. First time I've seen you laugh in a long while."

They walked on in silence for a few moments.

"I'm thinking of chucking it in, Alan. I think it's time."

Grant stopped dead.

"Mac, you can't be serious?"

It was the first time he had not addressed his boss as "Sir" and he wondered if Mac had noticed.

Mac put his hand on Grant's shoulder.

"Alan, you've been a good friend, as well as a cracking officer, but I think it's time I went. The job's changing too much. Less about police work and more about stats. An old bugger like me needs to move to one side and let one of you youngsters have a go."

Grant shook his head.

"Sir, we still need people like you, ones with a nose for a villain."

Mac smiled. "You've got a pretty good nose yourself."

As they walked on, Grant felt an overwhelming sadness.

CHAPTER FIFTY-FIVE
4th July 1990, Hatton Gardens, London

"What do you think?"

"I would suggest you get a forensic team in as soon as it is safe. We're still damping down at the moment but shouldn't be too long. Then we can see if it's safe to enter. Considering the tenants of the building I can see no reason for it to burn the way it did. Our own guys are already here waiting to get in."

"I'll get SOCO down here right away. Pity about all the water."

"If you can think of a better way to put out a fire, lad, please feel free to have a go."

"Oh no...you play with the fires and we catch the bad guys. That's the deal."

DC Conroy and ADO Murphy were looking at the remains of a building in Hatton Wall. The building had been well alight when the Fire Service had arrived, and despite their best efforts the blaze had completely destroyed the three-storeys. It was a hard fight to stop it spreading along the row. The narrow street made things more difficult, and for their own safety, the Fire Service decided to let the building go, concentrating on saving the adjoining properties.

"What could make it burn like that?"

"I would hazard a guess some sort of chemical was involved in the initial explosion. The fire took hold quickly, but we won't know what caused it until SOCO and our investigators get involved. We may never know as the evidence may have washed away, but usually we can get traces from somewhere."

"Do we know if there was anyone in the building?"

"As far as we know everyone was out before we got here. The pawnbroker called it in. The explosion occurred on the top floor and up it went. He saw someone leaving shortly before, but he has no idea if anyone else was in there. That's the old boy over there, white-haired guy, Mr Ellison."

"Thanks. I suppose I better start doing my job now."

"That's what you get paid the big money for, lad," said the ADO.

"Who's been spreading those rumours?" Conroy laughed.

He walked over to where the dejected pawnbroker stood.

"Afternoon, Sir. I'm Detective Constable Conroy. I can see you are in a bit of shock but I need to ask you a few questions while things are still fresh in your mind. Fancy a drink?"

"I would normally say it's a bit early for me detective, but looking at this mess, I'll take you up on it."

The Hat and Tun public house was a short walk away, along Hatton Wall. Conroy knew this area and its history well. There had been a pub here since the eighteenth century, and judging by the look of some of the faces in here, some of the customers had been there since the day the original pub opened. He took the drinks over to a table in the corner where the pawnbroker sat. The old boy still looked shaken.

"Here, get that down you," Conroy said, putting a triple Scotch in front of him. "It won't change anything but you'll have a nice rosy glow about you".

"Thanks. I'm still shaking."

Conroy took out his notebook and started writing. Sometimes it was best to just listen, let the whole story come out on its own, and then ask the questions to fill in the gaps.

The old man described how he was cleaning the inside of the shop window when he heard a loud bang and glass falling into the street from the floors above. He rushed outside to see the top floor ablaze. He phoned the fire brigade from a neighbouring shop.

"Who had the top floor?"

"Harry Hart, a diamond dealer. Everyone knew him as Clark."

"Why's that?"

"On account of him looking like Superman. Well not dressed as Superman, but as the reporter who becomes Superman"

"Clark Kent?"

"That's the one."

"Was Mr Hart in the offices?"

"I don't know. Come to think of it, I haven't seen him around for a little while but he often disappears for a few weeks at a time."

"When was the last time you saw him?"

The old man let out a long sigh. "Must have been at least a week ago, if not longer. Days all merge together now. It's all gone you know, everything. My whole life has gone."

He looked at Conroy, his eyes filling with tears. "It was my father's shop, not even the Germans managed to destroy it in the war, and now this." His eyes had a faraway look as he gazed down at the drink in his hand. The trembling sent ripples through the amber liquid.

Conroy waited a minute before asking, "So you can't say whether anyone was in the offices then?"

"No."

"What about the men you saw leaving?" asked Conroy.

"There were two of them."

"Did you see them go in?"

The old man considered for a moment then replied, "No, but I'd only just gone into the window. I was giving it a clean and rearranging some of the displays."

"So they must have been in there before you went into the window?"

"Yes, they must have been." He paused, "Does that mean Clark was in the office when the fire started?" he asked.

"We won't know for a while if anyone was in there."

"I hope he wasn't. He was a nice man."

"Can you describe the men who came out?"

"Rough-looking, you know, hard men. Not the sort you would like to see coming into the shop."

"What were they wearing?" continued Conroy.

"They were well-dressed. One was in a suit and the other had an overcoat, you know, those wool ones, expensive."

"Crombie?"

"Yes, a Crombie. Black."

"The men or the coat?"

"Oh, the coat. The men were white."

"Can you remember anything else about them, such as height and build?"

"One was really short, the man in the coat. Couldn't have been more than five foot two. The other must have been around six feet."

"Would you recognise them again?"

"Maybe. I don't know. I only caught a glimpse of them."

Conroy reached into his top pocket, pulled out a business card and handed it to the old man.

"If you think of anything, anything at all please give me a call. It doesn't matter how trivial it may seem. You never know what it might lead to."

The old man stared at the card and then slowly looked up at Conroy. "What will I do now? That place was my life."

"Is there anyone I can contact, you know, to come and take you home?"

"No, no one."

Conroy reached for his radio and, after a brief conversation with the control room, told the old man a couple of uniformed officers would come to pick him up and give him a lift home.

The old man lifted his head and looked at Conroy, slowly nodding once to acknowledge.

Conroy's last view as he left the pub was of him staring into the distance, the part filled glass still in his hand.

Minutes later, back at the scene of the fire ADO Murphy spotted Conroy and came straight over.

"You are definitely going to need SOCO now lad. We've found a body, or to be more precise we have found some charred remains of what used to be part of a body."

"Bloody marvellous," said Conroy, "looks like I won't be making it to White Hart Lane this afternoon then."

"There's always something to be thankful for, eh lad?" the ADO said laughing.

CHAPTER FIFTY-SIX

5th July 1990, Peterhead, Aberdeenshire

"Sir, have you seen this?"

DS Grant dropped a fax in front of Mac. He picked it up and quickly scanned through it. He put it down and ran his hand through his hair.

"So they have a body, but they are only surmising it's Hart because it was from his office?"

"Yes, sir. Too badly burned from the fire. They're fairly sure it was oxyacetylene cutting equipment that went up."

"Why on earth would Hart have cutting equipment? As far as we've established he was a straightforward diamond dealer. Not a hint of anything dodgy at all. Any chance this could have been a burglary?"

"That's what I thought, Sir. So I gave this DS Bell a call. Seems it was their first thought too, but since the fire, there's not been a trace of Hart. That's why they're thinking this might be him."

"It doesn't make any sense, Grant. A diamond dealer is burnt in his own offices whilst trying to break into his own safe. Why didn't he call in a locksmith if he had lost his keys?"

"I agree. Not sure the Met do though, Sir. They're under a lot of pressure to mark this one as solved. Keeps the figures looking good."

"Jesus. When are the politicians going to learn we're here to nab villains, not support their careers by producing meaningless statistics no one believes except themselves?"

"I'm not sure they even believe them, Sir."

"Well, it's about time they took a good, long, hard look at policing in this country. They expect us to do this job with one hand tied behind our back, and in the other a pen, filling in bloody mindless paperwork."

Grant was beginning to regret mentioning the pressure the Met were under. Once Mac got started on political intervention, there was no knowing how long he would vent his frustration. Today was an exception.

"Enough ranting. How does this affect our investigation?" asked Mac.

"I don't see as it makes any difference, to be honest. We haven't been able to prove any sort of connection between the two lads and any of the others. Apart from the circumstantial evidence tying them to the helicopter, and the fact we know they were in the area at the time of the robbery, we don't have a thing to prove they were involved at all. I can't see how they would have found out about the diamonds in the first place. I still think we're looking at a third party who set this thing up. They may have been involved in helping with the helicopter theft but at the moment I don't see how we can prove it."

Mac mulled this over then said, "Okay. If we can't prove they were involved, can we eliminate them?"

"I think we might have to, at least for the time being. We need to find the link, someone who knew the deal was about to take place."

"This might put a different perspective on things," said Mac, holding up the fax. "If it was Hart who died in the fire then maybe we're looking at him being involved in some way, and because the robbery failed, someone's not too happy about it. Maybe our Mr Munro. I want you to get back on to this Sergeant What's-his-name and tell him we don't believe this was an accident. I'll get onto the Chief, and see if we can apply some pressure of our own to keep this open. Screw the politicians and their stats. When you've done that, we'll pull in the two lads and give them a proper squeeze this time, see what pops out."

CHAPTER FIFTY-SEVEN
6th July 1990, Stuartfield, Aberdeenshire

"Stephen Hayling, I have a warrant for your arrest and to search your house and vehicles. I'm arresting you on suspicion of theft and attempted robbery. You do not have to say anything, but anything you do say may be noted in evidence." DS Grant was in Steve's living room with four uniformed officers when he cautioned Steve. He noted the look of absolute shock on Steve's face.

"I don't understand," Steve said. "Theft of what? Who am I supposed to have robbed? I haven't robbed anyone."

"In that case you have nothing to worry about. We're going to conduct the search first then we'll go down the nick, and you and me are going to have a nice little chat about what you were up to the other week."

Two of the officers started to search the house while the other two went out to the garage.

A short time later one of the officers returned from the garage. "Where are your Land Rover keys?"

Steven nodded towards the sideboard. "In the bowl."

The officer took the keys and went back outside.

"What's all this about?"

"We'll discuss that down at the station. Shouldn't be much longer here."

"It would help if I knew what you were looking for."

Grant smiled at Steve.

Finally the officer returned to the living room.

"Anything?" asked Grant.

"Nothing in the house," said one of the officers.

"Nothing out of the ordinary in the garage either. No evidence of spray equipment though there is a compressor."

"What are you looking for?" asked Steve.

"We'll discuss that at the station," repeated Grant.

Steve was led out to an unmarked police car and put into the back. At least he had been spared handcuffs.

The drive to Peterhead police station took twenty minutes. Grant took Steve to the custody sergeant and explained the circumstances of the arrest.

He left Steve at the desk. Once he had been processed, Steve would be escorted to one of the interview rooms. Grant and Mac were going to conduct the interview, or rather Grant was. Mac was letting him run with this one. They had some evidence which pointed a finger at Steve and Andy and the only real way to clear it up was to interview them both. DI Kerr collected Andy from his home address and conducted his interview at the same time in Aberdeen's Queen Street Police Station. Grant collected a folder from his desk and Mac joined him as he went to the interview room.

The room was small. There were no windows, illumination coming from a single light bulb. It was furnished with a desk and four chairs. Steve sat in one of the chairs and a uniformed officer stood by the door.

Grant and Mac sat down opposite Steve. Grant opened a twin pack of tapes and inserted them both in the tape recorder at the end of the desk.

He explained the purpose of the tapes and what would happen to them once the interview had finished.

"Interview with Stephen Hayling. Present in the room are Detective Chief Inspector MacIntyre and myself Detective Sergeant Grant. Stephen, we want to ask you a few questions regarding your whereabouts last month. Notably between the 18th and the 21st of June. I must remind you that you are under caution and do not have to say anything, but anything you say may be used against you."

"Okay, but I really don't know how I can help you."

"Let's start with the theft of the helicopter. What can you tell me about your involvement in that?"

"Involvement? I came back on shift and found out we had a Bolkow stuck out on the Kyle Invermoriston road. I was sent up to change a boost pump. That's all I know."

"So you're saying you don't know anything about the theft? You didn't help take it?"

"Help who?"

"I don't know, you tell me."

"I don't have anything to tell." Steve looked at the two detectives, with a look of bewilderment.

"Have you ever been to Ceannacroc?"

"Aye."

"Recently?"

"Aye, about two months ago. Me and my mate Andy take the dirt bikes up past into the hills there sometimes."

"Andy who?"

"Mannion."

"You haven't been there more recently, say, last month?"

"No, not to Ceannacroc itself. Been along the road past it."

"Why were you there?"

"We were camping at Balmacara. Fishing trip."

"But you didn't stop at Ceannacroc? Do you know the old barn there?"

"Aye, up past the power station intake. I know it. Why?"

"Ever been inside it?"

"Yes, once, we got caught out in a storm, we went in to shelter while it passed. Why are you asking me about the barn? We didn't steal anything from there if that's what you mean. There's nothing there to steal."

"When was that?"

"About two months ago, last time we were up there. Look what's this all about?"

"You sure you weren't there more recently, in a Land Rover?"

"We never take the Land Rover up there. We leave it near the village and go up on the bikes."

Steve looked at the two detectives in turn. "Can you tell me what this is about?"

Grant glanced at Mac. There was an imperceptible shake of the head.

"All in good time, just please answer the questions."

"Wait a minute. You said theft and robbery. You think I had something to do with stealing YZ?"

"Did you?"

"No. How could I? I wasn't even here."

"Your prints are on the controls, and in the cabin."

"Are you serious? I work on it, for Pete's sake. Of course my prints are on it, and every other helicopter based at Longside."

"So where were you?"

"I told you in my statement, when we came back. I was on the west coast, fishing. Andy was with me, he can vouch for me, and I have a receipt for the campground at Balmacara."

"Who do you know in London?"

"What? Why are you asking about London?"

"Know anyone there?"

"Not as far as I remember, no."

"You have to tell us the truth, Stephen."

"I am telling you the truth." Steve dropped his head and paused for a few seconds. "Okay, here's the truth. I don't have a clue why you think I had something to do with this."

There was a knock at the door and a constable popped his head in and spoke to Mac, "Sir, could I have a quick word?"

Mac slipped out of the door but returned almost immediately. He sat down and showed Grant a piece of paper.

Grant smiled, "Because we have evidence that tells us you did."

CHAPTER FIFTY-EIGHT
6th July 1990, Peterhead, Aberdeenshire

"What do you mean, 'evidence'?"

"Why have you got remnants of white paint on your Land Rover Stephen?"

"Because it's a bugger to get off that's why."

"What's it doing there in the first place?"

"It was hired by a film production company and they wanted it painted up as a UN vehicle."

"Why yours in particular?"

"Because it happened to be parked next to a Gazelle I was looking after, they had already hired."

"It's not looking too good, Stephen," Grant chipped in. "The barn, the fingerprints, and now this."

Steve shook his head. "I don't know where you're going with this but I seriously doubt we're going to get there."

"We're going to get to the bottom of it."

"There's nothing to get to the bottom of."

"Tell me about the phone call from London."

"What phone call?"

"April 17th, you had a call from a London call box."

"You're asking me to remember a phone call from April, you are joking right?"

"I don't joke, Stephen."

"I can believe that." Steve muttered.

"We're not here to talk about me. Just tell me who else was involved."

"I can't tell you who was involved because I have no idea what anyone was involved in. Other than what you've told me I haven't the foggiest what you're talking about."

"Right. Let's start at the beginning shall we? What do you know about the theft of a helicopter from Longside?"

After spending another two hours going over the story, it was clear Steve was sure about what he was saying. No amount of trying had caught him off-guard, and it worried Grant. He had a feeling the story was too tight. He felt there should have been more hesitation from Steve, more uncertainty in his answers.

"Stephen, we have the evidence, why don't you just admit it. You were involved."

"What you're saying to me is you have evidence I have been in a barn, which I freely admitted and explained. You have evidence my Land Rover was once painted white, which I explained. My fingerprints are on a helicopter I work on. I was on leave and in the general vicinity of some sort of robbery. Oh, and I'm capable of flying a helicopter."

"Did you do it?"

"Do you seriously think I am capable of flying a helicopter into the mountains?"

"You tell me."

"Have you ever done any flying?" Steve countered. "Because if you had you would know there's a big difference between crashing in a simulator and crashing for real. You get to walk away from one but chances are you don't from the other."

"Risk versus reward, Stephen. You know that. You ride a motorcycle off road."

"Aye and if I crash it doesn't make a smoking hole in the ground...well not usually."

Steve leaned back in his chair and clasped his hands on his head. He looked at the two detectives.

"I don't know what more you want me to say. Yes, I was in the area, but as for the rest I don't know what you're talking about."

"How did you know to take a fuel pump to recover the helicopter?"

Steve sighed. "Because it's my job. The pilot who went to recover it told me he had no fuel pressure indicated. The engineer who went with him said he couldn't hear the pump running. Of course it could have been a lot of other things, but the pump would be my first choice every time. After the fuse that is, and I had one of them with me too."

Grant looked at Mac and raised an eyebrow. Mac gave a slight shrug of the shoulders.

"Interview terminated at 13.56." Grant switched off the tape. "Okay that's it Stephen, you're free to go."

"Really? You drag me down here, grill me for three hours and that's it?"

"You can stay if you have something to tell us."

Steve shook his head.

"The constable will escort you out."

Steve left without saying another word.

"What do you think, Sir? Grant asked.

"I think we have a lot of circumstantial which puts him in the general area, but nothing concrete. He has opportunity; Mannion has financial problems which gives us motive. On the other hand, he didn't deny any of it and had pretty viable explanations."

"That's what worries me. He had an answer for everything."

"Sometimes that's just the way it is. Check out the story about the paint. Not much we can do about the barn except tie it up with the guys in Aberdeen and see what Mannion had to say for himself. Speak to the pilots at Bond again and see if they think Hayling is really capable of carrying out the flight. Once we have those answers we'll take it from there."

"He was involved, Mac."

"We don't have enough to charge them with involvement in the theft, let alone for attempted robbery. We can't place them at the scene at the time. I was as close as you could get to the guy running to the helicopter. There is no way I could pull him out of a line up. Aye, maybe he was the same build as Mannion but that's all I could tell you. And if the ability to fly a helicopter makes you a suspect, we have to eliminate a lot more than those two from our enquiries."

"I know they were involved," Grant said.

"Knowing is one thing, proving it is a whole new trawler full of herring. The Procurator Fiscal likes his herring."

"And I'm pretty sure we are getting red ones here," answered Grant.

CHAPTER FIFTY-NINE
11th July 1990, Stuartfield, Aberdeenshire

The knock on the door woke Steve. He had been dozing in the chair in front of the TV. He was enjoying one of the few days off he'd managed since the interview. It was holiday season and several staff were on leave. So far he had been to the Forties field twice and the Fulmar once. Bond had several helicopters based offshore, and when they needed a hand guess who got called?

He opened the door and was surprised to see Andy there.

"I thought you were working?"

"I was, right up until the point they sacked me."

"What the hell for?"

"Gross misconduct. Seems whilst they turned a blind eye to me flying in the sim, they didn't like I took you flying too, even though they had known about it for some time."

"Bastards. Come in, I'll make a cuppa."

"You not got anything stronger?"

Steve led Andy into the living room. "Scotch?"

"Ordinarily I'd say no, but right now..."

Steve poured two generous measures of Glenmorangie. "Here. Get that down your neck."

"I don't know what I'm going to do now. No money, no job and soon nowhere to live."

CHAPTER SIXTY
11th July 1990, Wapping, London

Nicky was not happy. A man who came from nowhere had persuaded him to do as he was told. Nicky didn't think this was the first time he had done this either. Before he knew what was happening he was hustled into the outer office of Munro Diamonds.

"Caught him snooping around outside, Mr Munro. Thought you might want a little chat with him, like. What with losing Eddie like that, thought he might have something to do with it, like. Know what I mean, Mr Munro."

Nicky hadn't wanted to get so close to Donald Munro but the gun pressed into the small of his back had changed his mind. Even though he was ready to lose the contents of his stomach, through either end, he didn't really care which, he couldn't help but notice Munro's sumptuously decorated offices.

"I see."

Donald looked at Nicky whilst addressing his captor.

"This gentleman and I are going to have a wee chat, so if you don't mind waiting outside, Willie, where you can be handy, if you get my drift."

"Very good, Mr Munro, if you say so."

Donald rolled his eyes and sighed. "Yes, Willie — I just said so."

"Now then Mr err..."

"Rolands, Nicky Rolands."

"Well, Nicky, you're going to tell me all about why you were snooping around, and then you're going to tell me everything you know about anything. And you have to hope I like your story, so make it a good one."

Munro led him into the inner office. If the outer office was well furnished then this was positively palatial.

Nicky had suffered a few setbacks in his relatively short life and been a bit too close to some nasty people once or twice, but now he was inside the offices of Donald Munro. He was smooth and pleasant enough on the outside, but Nicky had grown up close enough to this area to know the Munro the streets knew. He was really deep in it this time, and to make matters worse he had not told a soul where he was going. How could he be so stupid?

His editor knew he was in London, following up on the link between Lenny, Munro and the man he still couldn't place, but he had not told anyone he was going to snoop around Munro's offices. Even Nicky wasn't sure why he was there. Perhaps he was hoping to get a glimpse of someone who would break the story wide open. Instead he found himself in the offices of one of the most notorious gangland bosses in London.

"Take a seat, Nicky. Now, let's start at the beginning."

Nicky related all the events that led him here, from following up on the theft of the helicopter, to seeing Lenny at

Inverness. Despite his nerves he found himself presenting the story well. He even imagined himself narrating it in a documentary. He didn't tell it all of course. He left out the part about how he knew Lenny worked for Munro, and how he persuaded his editor to follow his nose and come to London.

Munro listened without interruption until Nicky had finished, then got up and started to walk around the room. When he walked behind his chair Nicky became alarmed but Munro continued until he stopped in front of him. He was not a tall man but Nicky found him menacing.

Nicky's mouth was dry and he was still shaking. He hoped he'd said enough for Munro to be satisfied and let him go.

There was a long silence broken only by the ticking of an antique bracket clock on a nearby table. Not even the sounds of the river could be heard in the room.

When Munro spoke, he spoke softly.

"So how did you know this...ah...Lenny fellow?"

"Are you saying you don't know him, Mr Munro? I thought he worked for you."

"Did you indeed? I am not saying anything Nicky. I ask the questions and you give me the answers. At least that's what I thought I agreed at the beginning."

Nicky realised he had made a mistake. He had been clever leaving that part out and now he had given it away on the first question. He shouldn't have been surprised Lenny would be the first thing Munro would ask about. Nicky hadn't been thinking straight. Why else would he have come to Munro's offices if he didn't know he worked for him? Even though he knew he had given the game away, Nicky knew there was a story in here somewhere. So he continued to try to bluff his way.

"Sorry Mr, Munro. I thought..."

Donald held up his hand to Nicky.

"Nicky. Nicky, my friend. Let me do the thinking and you do the answering. That way I'll know what I need to know and you can get to leave here. The sooner the better, eh?"

Nicky nodded. "Lenny and I were at school together."

"Really? Now that is interesting. Tell me, where was that?"

"Langdon Park."

Munro raised his eyebrows as if he was surprised.

"The Langdon Park near Limehouse Cut?"

Nicky nodded.

"And you say saw this Lenny character at Inverness Airport? What were you doing there if you're an East End lad?"

Nicky told Munro how he had finished up working for a paper in Aberdeen and where he was going when he spotted Lenny.

"And you're sure this man you saw in the airport is the same one you went to school with?"

"Yes, but surely if he works for you then you know he's from the East End?"

Munro ignored the question.

"Tell me more about this helicopter."

Nicky again related the story about the stolen helicopter and the events at the Cluanie Inn, where he had followed Lenny and the other man the night before.

"Look, Mr Munro, I already told you this."

Munro rubbed his hands over his face. Nicky thought he looked tired and a little concerned.

"And you are sure this man is the one you went to school with in the East End?"

Nicky nodded. "Yes, I'm positive."

CHAPTER SIXTY-ONE

11th July 1990, Stuartfield, Aberdeenshire

"You're not going to be on the streets, Andy. You can move here until we get something sorted."

"I can't do that."

"Yes, you can, and you will. Tomorrow I'll see about renting a truck from Turners and we'll get you out of there."

Andy surprised Steve when he suddenly burst into tears. "Where the hell did it all go wrong? I'm a mess. I can't take much more of this. All this suspicion is driving me up the wall. I need to get out of it."

"Jeez, Andy, don't set me off. It's going to be Okay. You'll have a roof over your head and food on the table."

They sat in silence for a few minutes then Steve said, "You know what? It's time for a move. I'm going to put the house on the market and you and me are going to bugger off away from all this."

"What? Now?" exclaimed Andy.

"Yeah. I'm sick of it too. There's a cloud hanging over me at work as well and I know I've got someone tailing me."

"Really?"

"Yeah, I've caught sight of a car a couple of times so I've driven home via all sorts of strange routes. Must really be pissing him off."

Andy burst out laughing. "You are totally and utterly nuts."

"I hope so, mate, and I intend staying that way. Anyway, where do you fancy going?"

"For a trip, or forever?"

"Forever. It's time we moved on".

CHAPTER SIXTY-TWO
11th 1990, Wapping, London

Munro stood looking at Nicky for a few moments, which to Nicky seemed to last forever. He was deciding what to do with him, of that Nicky was sure. Well, he'd told him the truth, and as far as Nicky could tell, neither Munro nor Lenny had done anything wrong. He didn't see any reason why he wouldn't be shown the door and be on his way.

Munro seemed to make up his mind and summoned Willie back.

"Willie, Mr Rolands here has been most co-operative. As a reward I would like you to take him for a big drink, settle his nerves. Make sure he gets the full works. You know the ropes."

Nicky wasn't sure what had just happened but it seemed Munro had been happy with their chat.

"Sure thing Mr Munro, the place down the river?"

"Yes, that's the one, it's a quiet place, and you can get to know each other a little better."

In his relief at being allowed to go Nicky had missed the nuances in the conversation between Donald and his minion. He was just glad to be getting out of here. He was told to wait with another of Munro's men whilst Willie brought the car to the front entrance.

Willie got out of the car and motioned to the other man to take the wheel, then signalled Nicky to get into the back of the Daimler. Willie got in beside him. As they pulled away Nicky started to replay the last few minutes in his head. Something about this wasn't right.

As he turned towards Willie to ask him where they were going, the fist caught him on the side of the chin, slamming his head into the side window. Dazed, he was vaguely aware of his hands being yanked behind his back and being bound with a rough material. This couldn't be happening. Mr Munro had said he should be taken for a drink.

Then it dawned on him. They were going to throw him in the river. He tried to speak, but another blow to the face stopped him and he was vaguely aware of the gaffer tape being applied to his mouth. He could feel the trickle of blood from his cut lip and he became afraid he would choke on his own blood before they got to the river. A hood went over his head.

"Stay still and don't make a sound or you will truly know the meaning of pain, if you know what I mean."

Nicky had no intention of doing anything other than he was told. He did not like pain, especially his own, and his youth made him optimistic he would still find a way to get out of this, one way or another.

CHAPTER SIXTY-THREE
11th July 1990, Wapping, London

As soon as Nicky had been taken away, Donald picked up the phone and dialled someone he had not spoken to for a while.

"Charles, how the devil are you keeping?"

"Well, well, well, if it isn't the mightiest Scottish Munro of them all."

Charlie McBride was a contemporary of Donald Munro. He too had grown up in Glasgow in the Fifties and Sixties. Charlie had arrived in London a bit later than Donald and had taken care not to step on Donald's turf. He had always referred to Donald as the mightiest Munro, a reference to the tall peaks of Scotland.

Donald laughed.

"Do ye never tire of that one, Charlie?"

"Aye ye ken how it is. The old ones are the best, just like me and you, Donald. What can I do you for?"

"It's a bit delicate, Charlie. It seems like one of my boys might have been a bit naughty."

Donald explained how he was down two and a half million dollars. He didn't explain the circumstances of how the money was lost, other than he had a business partner who had conveniently disappeared. Even if they had a lot of history together, he still didn't want one of the other gangland bosses knowing all of his business. Especially when they could easily muscle in on the deal.

"So where do I come in?"

"The only other person involved was Lenny, and it appears Lenny has been telling porkies. Not only that but I hav'nae seen hide nor hair of him since last week."

"Lenny? Your Lenny? Lenny who couldn't count above ten with his shoes on? You serious?"

"Hard to believe I know, but as he was the only other person involved with the deal, I can't rule him out."

"You don't seem to be having much luck, Donald, what with Eddie's accident and now this."

Donald paused and brushed his hand over his hair.

"How do you know about Eddie?"

"Oh, you know how it is. One of your lads bumped into one of mine. Got to chatting about this and that, and out it comes. Eddie blew himself up."

"I would rather you keep that under your hat if you don't mind."

"Aye, Okay. So, like I said, how can I help?"

"I want you and the lads to keep an eye out for Lenny, and if you find him bring him to me, in one piece, well breathing at least."

CHAPTER SIXTY-FOUR
11th July 1990, Wapping, London

"Mike Papa...India Nine Nine."

"India Nine Nine, pass your message."

The Metropolitan Police Bell 222 helicopter orbited slowly at a thousand feet above Wapping. In this position the helicopter was almost directly in the flight path for London City Airport. The pilot liaised with Air Traffic Control, as one of the observers communicated with the Metropolitan Police Information Room and units on the ground.

"Three men entering a black Daimler saloon at the front of the target building. Nine Nine."

"Roger, Nine Nine, standby."

As the helicopter circled, the observer kept his camera trained on the target vehicle.

"Nine Nine from MP."

"Go ahead."

"Nine Nine, from Silver, stay with the vehicle."

The tactical commander of the operation had made the decision to task the Police helicopter to follow the car wherever it went. It would leave the ground operation with no 'eye in the sky,' but that was why operations like this had a command structure. Someone had to make the tactical decisions.

One observer passed information to the control room as the vehicle set off along Wapping High Street. The other observer kept the camera trained on the target.

The car turned onto the A13 and headed east. Seeing the direction the car was taking, the pilot contacted London City Airport Air Traffic Control again.

"City Approach, Police 252."

"Police 252 go ahead."

"Ah...252 one thousand feet, heading zero nine zero, north of Limehouse Basin and abeam this time. Tracking target eastbound on A13."

"Roger 252. Not above one thousand feet, remain to the north of the extended centreline. Report three DME if continuing. I have inbound traffic on a ten mile final. "

The London City Airport air traffic controller did his utmost to assist the Police helicopter and had given permission to approach within three miles of the runway. As long as the car remained on the A13 they would be able to pass to the north of the airport without drama. The controller's priority was the safety of the passenger flights in his control. If it meant stopping the helicopter from continuing its task then he would do so, and the police would have to wait.

Helicopter flying anywhere in London required a high level of concentration; working in close proximity of an airport presented its own set of problems. The pilot not only had to be able to keep track of the target but he also had to have situational awareness at all times. Flying into the wrong area at the wrong time could be catastrophic.

The observers also had to be aware of the target, as well as guide any necessary ground units. Flying in the Air Support Unit required a good sense of teamwork.

The Police observer co-ordinated ground units for a possible interception on the A13 when the car unexpectedly turned right heading towards the river.

"MP, from Nine Nine. Do we have a river unit available?"

"Nine Nine, standby."

The pilot made a snap decision to move to the south side of the river to get a better view of the shoreline in the front.

"City Approach, 252."

"252, go ahead."

"Request clearance to cross centreline at East India Basin and work south of the river."

The air traffic controller decided there was enough time to allow the helicopter to fly past the end of the runway. The inbound traffic was at the opposite end but he had to keep the centreline clear in case the aircraft had to abort the landing for some reason.

"252 approved, expedite."

The pilot hoped the driver of the car below was not going to change his mind about going to the river. He was stuck south of the runway now until the incoming aircraft had landed.

"Nine Nine, Thames Division Tango Whisky One is available. Currently at Greenwich Pier."

"MP, roger. Request talk-through."

The observer needed to speak directly to the boat below, rather than relay his message through the information room. It would take the launch almost five minutes to travel the two miles downriver to where it appeared the car was headed. He quickly apprised the officers on the Police launch of the situation and requested assistance.

"Did you see that?" the observer asked.

"He doesn't look like he wants to go for a boat ride," the second observer commented.

"MP, India Nine Nine, urgent."

The observer informed the Information Room one of the passengers was being taken aboard the boat against his will. He then passed the same information to the launch, now making its way towards the wharf.

As the observers watched, the man got thrown into the bottom of the boat. The boat moved away from the pier as one of the men bound the prisoner's ankles with rope, finally attaching a length of anchor chain.

"I don't think they plan on bringing him back," noted the pilot. "I hope the launch can get to him in time. If they decide to dump him over the side, there's not a lot we can do about it."

CHAPTER SIXTY-FIVE
11th July 1990, River Thames, London

The car finally came to a halt in what sounded to be a gravel car park. Nicky was bundled out of the car. He could smell the sea. They must be near the estuary. The men led him a short distance to some steps. Metal. He was being taken onto a jetty of some sort. He could hear their feet on the metal gratings and the water lapping around the piles.

His hopes were raised a little. Maybe if they pushed him off he would be able to struggle ashore somehow. That idea was dashed as he was pushed headlong into the bottom of a boat. It stank of fish. From the movement of the boat he guessed it wasn't a big one. Probably one of the small trawlers that worked in the estuary.

The boat started up and pulled away from the jetty, Nicky was aware of his ankles being bound, then he heard a rattle. He didn't think he could be any more frightened than he already was, but the sound of the chain forced him into uncharted territory. Up until the chains he thought it might be possible to escape somehow, but now he realised his short life was about to end and he started to sob. The pain in his side was excruciating as the boot found its mark.

"Shut up or you'll get some more."

To Nicky it seemed to be a lifetime, his lifetime, until the motor stopped, but he knew it was probably no more than half an hour. He realised this was the end. What bothered him the most now was he had no idea where he was. He was going to his death and he didn't know where. What was worse, nobody else would know. He would disappear off the face of the earth. How could he be so stupid, not telling anyone where he was going? Hands grabbed him and he was roughly pulled to his feet. Somebody pulled the hood from his head and ripped the tape from his mouth.

The sudden light hurt Nicky's eyes.

CHAPTER SIXTY-SIX
11th July 1990, River Thames, London

"Tango Whisky One, Nine Nine."

"Nine Nine, go ahead."

The observer in the helicopter passed the information that one of the passengers had been bound with chains. They had managed to get the registration number of the boat, a fishing vessel, and were making checks on the ownership. In the meantime, the launch was ordered to intercept, as it had become a 'risk of life' situation.

The police launch had blue lights showing, but the Inspector switched them off. He didn't want the other vessel tipped off and have them dump the captive over the side.

Although the Inspector now knew the other ship was a fishing boat and probably capable of no more than ten knots, he knew they would still have a bit of a chase. He hoped the captors would head downriver, at least past the Thames Barrier, because by his reckoning by then they would catch up.

They were taking a chance going at this speed in the dark, and without the added protection of the blue lights. It was a life and death situation with a calculated risk. He was not going to risk their own lives needlessly.

"TW One, Nine Nine."

"Go ahead."

"Target next vessel in front."

"Roger Nine Nine."

"Turn off the nav lights Tom."

The inspector could make out the vessel in front of him, about two hundred yards ahead. The stern light shone bright white.

With their own lights off they would be invisible to the other boat, apart from their wake. Now with their reduced speed even that would be hard to see.

They were a hundred yards astern when the fishing boat began to slow. This wasn't the deepest part of the channel but it was the deepest in this area. It looked like the dumping spot for the unfortunate soul. For a moment the Inspector wondered if they might have already killed him and this was a body disposal. He hoped not.

"Keep your speed up and come up on the landward side. With a bit of luck they won't see us until it is too late."

"Sir."

As the launch came alongside a few yards from the starboard side of the fishing boat the Inspector could see two men dragging a third to the side of the boat. They pulled the hood from his head just as the inspector turned on the powerful searchlight.

CHAPTER SIXTY-SEVEN
11th July 1990, Wapping, London

The match flared in the shadows, briefly illuminating his face. It had been several years since he had given up smoking, but tonight was a time to have a celebratory cigar. He was confident he wouldn't be seen here in the doorway. Everyone across the street was far too busy to notice passers-by or casual watchers. The man in the shadows continued to watch as Donald Munro was led from the building by two large policemen, and bundled into a waiting patrol car. He was followed by several more officers leading what remained of Donald's minders to a line of police cars waiting behind. Standard police procedure; transport the suspects in separate vehicles so they can't confer and get their stories straight. Divide and conquer.

Pity they didn't get that arsehole Willie and his mate Peter. He never liked them. Shame about the kid too, whoever he was. He wouldn't be coming back. Not if those two had taken him somewhere in the car.

The watcher smiled. Still, they finally had Donald Munro, and he was going to reap what he had sown. As the police cars pulled away they left one solitary straggler, and an officer by the door. The watcher set off along the High Street. He had work to do.

CHAPTER SIXTY-EIGHT
11th July 1990, River Thames, London

"POLICE. STAY WHERE YOU ARE AND PREPARE FOR BOARDING".

The bright light was not coming from the boat he was on but a Police launch rapidly pulling alongside.

Nicky could not believe it was happening. He really was being rescued in the nick of time. He wished they'd been a few seconds earlier, before the involuntarily release of his bladder. He was acutely aware of the wetness in his crotch and running down his leg. Still, it was better than being wet all over and sinking to the bottom of the Thames.

The officers quickly boarded the fishing vessel and arrested the three other men in the boat. It was clear to them who the victim was. Not many people travel in boats with chains fastened to their ankles.

"Are you Okay?" one of the officers asked him.

Nicky shook his head.

"Not really," he replied. "I've never been so scared in my life. Where did you guys come from?"

The officer explained how Munro's place had been under observation for a raid, and the helicopter had seen the car leaving.

"I can't believe it," said Nicky. "You turned up like some super hero. . ." Nicky stopped.

"What is it?" asked the officer.

"Oh nothing," said Nicky.

In one of those perverse ways the mind works, Nicky had finally remembered where he had seen Lenny's companion before.

CHAPTER SIXTY-NINE
12th July 1990, Peterhead, Aberdeenshire

"Alan. Get your arse over here," Mac called out to Grant. He'd just put down the phone. He was grinning.

"What is it?"

"Some good news from the Met. Munro's been arrested. Conspiracy to murder and possession of counterfeit currency."

Grant let out a whoop of delight.

"At least someone has been nicked for something. Result!"

"Don't be bitter, Alan. At least the mean bastard is going away for a long stretch, assuming CPS let it go ahead of course. Seems watertight though. You'll never believe who he was having murdered."

Grant frowned and shook his head.

"Only Nicky bloody Rolands."

"You're kidding."

"Nope. Seems he was following this Morvern fellow and got a bit too close to Munro. He's been telling the Met all about it. Morvern seems to have double-crossed Munro somehow."

Grant cocked his head to one side.

"You think this is tied in somehow?"

"Can't see how it can't be. Too much of a coincidence. Morvern comes up here as part of a deal. Robbery goes wrong and Morvern disappears. Maybe he set it up."

"Aye, perhaps. But it still doesn't let those two off the hook. They could be part of the set-up."

"They could, Alan, but I think you'll have to let it go. We've only got the slightest of circumstantial. Mannion and Hayling are not acting like they did anything wrong, in fact just the opposite. Hayling has his house on the market but he doesn't seem to be in any hurry to leave. If they were in on it for a share, they dipped out, if they were paid cash for the job, well they aren't showing any signs of it."

"No, you're right...but..."

"I know. You have a good instinct, Alan, but it's not always right. I know, I've been there."

Grant sighed. "Yes, I suppose you're right." He looked at Mac. "Don't retire."

"We'll see. Times like these when there's a result, even if it isn't ours, I'm tempted to stay. But they don't seem to come as often now as they used to do."

Grant smiled. "Promise me you'll think about it."

Mac nodded. "I'll think about it. No promises mind."

CHAPTER SEVENTY

25th July 1991, Dickenson Bay, Antigua

"Well, well, well, look who it is. Detective Chief Inspector MacIntyre," said Steve.

He and Andy were relaxing at a table outside the Spinnaker Bar in Dickenson Bay, Antigua. Situated on the beach, the bar afforded a good view of the whole bay. An ideal place to spend a day just watching the world go by. All morning they had watched the cruise ships full of excited tourists heading for the entrance of St Johns Harbour. They would go home with tales of Caribbean Island life coloured by a morning visit to the tourist traps, as was always the way. Not that they felt any animosity towards them; tourist dollars were important to the island.

They were sipping rum and coke and looking relaxed.

"What brings you here?" asked Andy.

"A British Airways ticket," Mac replied dryly. "You see, I had a tip-off I would find two suspects in a helicopter theft and failed diamond robbery. I managed to persuade the boss, as I was coming up to retirement, I should perhaps take a holiday and combine business with pleasure. See if I could wrap up the case, even though we're not actively pursuing enquiries anymore. So here I am, and here you are."

Steve took another sip of his drink.

"How can you still suspect us? We answered all of your questions to your complete satisfaction." He smiled. "But you are wrong about us on one count, Chief Inspector."

"Oh am I now, and what would that be?"

"We didn't fail, Mac," Steve said quietly.

"What?" Mac stared at each of them in turn, bewilderment on his face. "The diamonds were dropped at the scene. I know, I picked up the bag and returned it to the Angolan fellow."

"The bag contained quartz pieces," said Andy.

"So this past year I've been thinking I was investigating the theft of a helicopter involved in a failed robbery, and all along it was a real robbery?"

"You were meant to think that, Mac. We wanted you to be able to report back you had foiled the robbery and the thieves had disappeared. We wanted you to believe it," said Steve as he handed the policeman an envelope.

"What's this?"

"Your share. A bank book and a new passport, in the same name as the bank book. You have a new life for your retirement. Drink, Mac?"

The policeman pulled up a chair and Steve signalled the waiter for more drinks. Andy excused himself and disappeared into the bar.

"So let me get this straight," said Mac. "You took the real diamonds and just went back to work as if nothing has happened? Even when arrested you just continued as if nothing had happened. Then a year later you two take a Caribbean holiday and get me to come out here to join you? What about the others, do they know about this?"

"Everyone has been squared, Mac," said Steve smiling. "We did it, we never stole the helicopter, just borrowed it. The diamonds were already stolen some might say, as they came from a mine UNITA had taken over the control of from the Angolan Government. We just diverted the funds to us, rather than to UNITA. We did a robbery that never was. No one is looking for us now. You have your retirement you thought you would never have in the package right there." Steve thought for a moment. "Well, almost no one is looking for us, except for maybe Munro and UNITA, though I am sure they'll never work out what really happened."

"Never mind them not having worked it out, I haven't either. Anyway, you needn't worry about Munro. He's not going to be looking for anyone for a while. Just back up a bit. We knew about Morvern and his connection to Munro, but the other chappie came up as a straight up diamond dealer. No record, not even a sniff of anything ropey. We thought he had perhaps hired the minder. So Munro was involved? Was that why the legit dealer was killed in a fire at his offices?"

Andy returned and gave a quick nod to Steve.

CHAPTER SEVENTY-ONE
25th July 1991, Cuito Cuanavale, Angola

Flies buzzed around his head but he couldn't swat them away. Any movement now would almost certainly be fatal. Some people thrived on it but for him there was only an overwhelming terror. He wasn't sure which was worse, not knowing whether this moment would be your last, or the thought of a long and painful death. And he was no stranger to pain anymore.

The enemy were close now, stealthily moving through the long grass towards their position. As soon as they were in the clearing he expected they would open fire. He hoped so. He would rather get on with it, get it over with.

After returning from London without the Major, Pereira had reported to the General. He told him of his suspicions prior to the operation and how he clearly had been justified in his thoughts. Of course he returned the diamonds. And that's when it all went wrong.

He had endured several months of "questioning", some of it more painful than others. What had he done with the real diamonds? His answer always the same. The diamonds had never been out of his sight. Never.

Finally they accepted his story. Wherever the diamonds were, he didn't know and had nothing to do with their loss. But that wasn't the end of it. He expected to return to his normal duties but Dr Savimbi was not a happy man. Unwittingly, he had cost UNITA a considerable sum of money and he had to be punished.

Although he was terrified, he still believed in the cause. Private Pereira had become a foot soldier, cannon fodder. But he knew they would understand one day. If he survived, he was certain he could redeem himself and return to his former duties. Private Pereira was not a complicated man. He would never understand human nature.

CHAPTER SEVENTY-TWO
25th July 1991, Dickenson Bay, Antigua

"Why is Munro no longer a problem? What happened?" asked Steve.

Mac spent the next few minutes recounting the events in London and Rolands' lucky escape.

"If that river unit had been a minute later we would never have found him..." Mac stopped speaking with his mouth still open.

Harry and Rachel had arrived at the bar.

"DCI MacIntyre, may I present the final two members of the team. Rachel MacInnes and Harry Hart, better known as Clark."

Mac shook his head as he looked at the pair.

"You're supposed to be dead. Harry Hart. I remember you well because I thought you looked like.....oh, Clark, now I see. And Rachel, you're the receptionist at the hotel. Was everyone in Scotland involved in this? I'm getting too old for this," he said. "Would someone mind telling me what really happened?"

"Clark here was the one who put together the deal with Munro."

Mac nodded.

Steve continued, "Clark is a legit merchant but he despises the fact that some of the other merchants don't care where the money is going."

Harry took over the story.

"Munro ripped me off when I was starting out. He didn't remember it because he's ripped off so many people over the years. I told him I would broker a meeting and invest in it myself. That persuaded Munro to join in. I chose the location for the meeting, with a little prompting from Steve. I told him the deal required three million, so Munro arranged half a million in cash and another two million in bearer bonds. The final half million was mine."

"So you pulled it off and netted three million dollars, I'm impressed."

Steve interjected.

"Eighteen and a half million dollars, Mac. Not bad for three months work eh?"

Mac almost choked on his drink, "Eighteen and a half million! How? You told me they were only asking three million for the diamonds."

"The diamonds had been grossly undervalued for a quick sale. The true value was more like six million. They were the real deal though. Clark had all the details and photographs of the diamonds, and had a good look at them on the day. Had they been fake or poor quality we would have aborted the whole thing. But we knew they weren't fake right from the start."

"How could you know for sure?"

"Because the seller, as you know, was José Duarte de Oliviera Silva, Ollie to his friends. He's a Major in UNITA, or he was. Clark here knows Ollie pretty well, he used to buy diamonds from him when Ollie worked at one of the Angolan mines. When he phoned Clark to discuss a deal he treated him as if he was only a vague acquaintance, so Clark knew he wasn't able to talk freely. He also knew if Ollie said the diamonds were good, then they were good. When Clark asked for the details to be faxed through, Ollie faxed them personally and was able to send an extra page. He let Clark know he wanted to get out of Angola and he felt this was a chance.

"So was he in on this?" asked Mac.

"He wasn't in on the planning, but he was in on the deal with an equal share. Once the robbery had failed and you had finished your questioning, Ollie and the Lieutenant left the Cluanie as soon as possible. You and Munro's muscle man just assumed they wanted to put as much distance between themselves and the police, as the diamonds had not been officially imported. Well, that was true, but Ollie also needed to get back to London to lose the Lieutenant. As soon as Pereira was out of the way, Ollie collected a package Harry had left at reception. There was enough money to tide him over for a while and a ticket to Lisbon. He already had his Portuguese passport with him, Ollie has dual nationality. UNITA was never aware he was mixed race so would have no idea where to look for him."

"And they would be looking for him because the bag of diamonds was now a bag of worthless quartz," said Mac.

"Exactly. I do feel sorry for him though. For the past twelve months he's been totally unaware of our success, but as of tomorrow he will know."

"He didn't know?"

"No. We couldn't let him in on the whole plan. We knew he would be questioned and we wanted him to act naturally."

Mac shook his head. "How did you get from six million to over eighteen?"

"Harry knows his onions, and even his diamonds. Once these were cut and polished they brought in a cool sixteen million."

Mac let out a long whistle. "Not that I want to correct you on such a trifling difference, but you said eighteen and a half was the final figure."

"Not only did we get the diamonds, but we took the money and bearer bonds too."

Mac intervened, "I handed those back too!"

"You remember the case thrown at you from the helicopter?"

"How could I forget? I wasn't expecting it. It nearly hit me in the face."

"Sorry, Mac," said Andy. "It had to look real though."

"It was a duplicate case." Steve continued. "We already knew what it looked like and the combination because Clark told us what he had supplied to Munro. In our case only the first and last note of each bundle was real, the rest were photocopies, enough to fool anyone giving it a casual glance. Munro's minder thought the money was safe when you spoke to him. He would only find out it was fake when he got back to London. Munro had put almost all of the money up front. It was part of the deal Clark negotiated. He had offered a seventy-thirty split if Munro would do that, and take the rest of Clark's contribution out of the profits. He couldn't resist the temptation."

"No wonder he was pissed-off then, if he lost two and a half million dollars. What about the body in the offices then? Who was it if it wasn't Clark?"

"We don't know. Clark was in Antwerp at the time and read about it in the English papers. He took the opportunity to disappear. It does mean most people think Clark is dead now though."

"I can tell you it was an oxyacetylene fire. Pretty intense by all accounts. That's why they couldn't identify the body." Mac ran his hand over his receding hairline.

"We did wonder why Ha...err...Clark was trying to break into his own safe. Our initial thoughts were it was someone else, but when there was still no trace of Harry we and the Met assumed it was him. Now I know it wasn't Clark I have to wonder if it was Morvern, he's not been seen since either, but then again he could be in the Thames if he lost Munro all that money."

Mac sat there slowly shaking his head then ran his hand across his hair.

"If you got away with the diamonds and the money how did you get rid of them? We were watching you all the time."

"Posted them at Invermoriston. The case went in a cardboard box and the diamonds in a jiffy envelope."

"You trusted them to the post?"

"We did pay for Special Delivery," Andy said laughing.

"Hell, Steve. That was a pretty audacious plan, and I thought I'd screwed it up with my timing. You know, getting a little too close. Just one more question though, I can't help it, I am a detective after all."

Steve smiled and nodded.

"How did you get to meet all these people in such a short time and get them to agree? You only had two months to pull it all together."

"Same way as I got to know you Mac. Fishing. Every person I met through fishing. Well, one I didn't but the rest I did. They were unhappy with their lives and I'd already established they would do pretty much anything to change it. Casual conversation, that was all. When the job came up they were all up for it. I must admit, I wasn't really sure you would go along, but something inside told me you really wanted a way out. I took the chance of telling you and getting banged up."

"I didn't know which way it would go either," Mac said. "You nearly did get banged up. But then I got to thinking about my dreams and thought, hell, why not?"

"I thought you had changed your mind when we were arrested. You could have warned us."

"Ah, now you see you're not the only one to keep surprises. If I'd warned you beforehand you wouldn't have had the look of shock on your face when you were arrested."

"Touché, Mac."

"What did you do with the wheels off the Land Rover, and all the other gear?" asked Andy.

"It was a tricky one," said Mac, "I had to put them somewhere where no one would think of looking. You never did see my new rock garden did you?"

"You buried the stuff in your own garden?" Steve asked.

"Don't think anyone is ever going to look there, do you?" asked Mac. "You said you met everyone except one through fishing. Who was the one person you didn't meet through fishing then?"

"Rachel. I suppose I did meet her through fishing in a roundabout way, but only because I stopped at the hotel one day for a break. We started dating. She was my girlfriend for quite some time, Mac, but not anymore."

"You still seem to be pretty close," said Mac looking at Rachel leaning her head on Steve's shoulder.

"I don't really have a choice," said Steve. "She made me marry her."

"I did not!" protested Rachel, sitting up straight. "You volunteered!"

"Of course I did, dear," said Steve, blowing her a kiss.

Rachel stuck her tongue out at him.

"Anyway, she had to be involved. It was mainly her idea," Steve said.

"Don't look so shocked, Mac. I can call you Mac now can't I?" asked Rachel.

Mac nodded.

"Steve is being modest. He was involved in it too, especially the planning."

"Yes. I was the bus driver."

"Ach, you know you were more than that." She pecked him on the cheek.

Mac sat there for a minute and then he slid the envelope back to Steve.

"I can't take it."

Steve sat up straight, "Why not?"

"I gave it a lot of thought. I was relieved in a way, when I thought it had all gone wrong. I've never taken money in my entire life. When I had that feeling after the robbery, I knew it was not right for me. And just now, when you handed me the envelope, it felt wrong."

"Mac, it's a hell of a lot of money you're turning down."

"I know but I really couldn't live with myself if I took it."

"So you going to turn us in?" asked Andy.

It seemed to be an eternity before Mac let out a sigh and said, "No. I went into this willingly, and just because I've changed my mind about the money, it doesn't mean I'm going to change my mind about helping. Damn, it was fun."

"You said you were about to retire? I thought you had another year to do? What happened?"

Mac let out a snort. "Yes, I do have another year, but this new Chief Constable and I don't get on. He's all about statistics and performance markers. I'm all about nicking villains so we've mutually agreed an early retirement. Oh, I know this money would give me what I want, but I really wouldn't be happy. I've sold the house, and between that and the insurance money from Helen, I've bought a smaller yacht for the Med. Can't do a world cruise but the Med is a big place."

"Costa Del Crime?"

"Bugger that. I put quite a few of them away. I don't want to wake up with the fishes. No, I'm going to the other end, maybe Italy and Sicily and definitely Greece and into the Aegean."

"And there's nothing we can do to change your mind?"

"No, Steve. I've never been more sure about anything in my life."

Steve nodded slowly. "Okay, Mac. Will you at least stay for another drink?"

"Thought you'd never ask. You don't think they do butteries here do you?"

CHAPTER SEVENTY-THREE
26th July 1991, Albufeira, Portugal.

"José!"

The shout came from the bar. It was Natanael, the owner.

"Que?"

"There is someone on the phone for you, says it is importante."

"What does he want?"

"He says he only speak to you."

José put down the filleting knife and washed the slime and blood from his hands. The freshly landed fish had barely stopped moving by the time they arrived in his kitchen at the restaurant. José loved to cook and hoped one day he would be able to open a restaurant of his own. Not that he would ever have the money. Not now. Things had not worked out for him as he had planned. Still, Natanael was a fair boss and he was content.

The telephone receiver was resting on the bar counter.

"Sim."

"Good morning. Is this Mr Silva?" The voice was soothing; quiet and relaxed. José suspected this man was in his later years.

"I am he."

"Mr Silva. I am Eduardo Gonzales of Gonzales and Barros solicitors in Portimão. Can you please confirm to me your name and date of birth?"

"What is this about?"

"I can only tell you that if you can confirm to me the details I have here."

"I am not sure I want to give my details to someone I don't know."

"I can assure you if you are the person I suspect you to be, it really is in your best interests."

José had no idea why a solicitor would be want to speak to him, but he didn't see any harm in just those details. Few people knew of his existence here. Let alone a firm of solicitors.

"I am José de Silva I was born on the 18th of June 1965."

"Thank you, Mr Silva. Thank goodness I have found you. I need you to come into the office to discuss an important matter. I cannot discuss it over the phone."

"You can hardly expect me to drop everything and come to Portimão on a whim."

"Indeed not, Mr Silva, but I have specific instructions I can only reveal this in person to you. Should you have any doubts about the veracity and integrity of our business please look us up in the phone book and call me back."

José did exactly that. He wasn't about to run around the country just on the say so of someone on the phone.

"Are you satisfied now, Mr Silva?"

"I am satisfied you are who you say you are, but I have no idea why you would want to see me. It is going to be difficult for me to get to you and do my work. I don't have a car and the bus journey would mean I would not be back in time to cook this evening."

"I fully understand, Mr Silva, which is why I will be sending you a chauffeur-driven limousine. Please make sure you bring your passport with you for a final verification of your identity."

José was speechless for a moment.

"It is that important?"

"Even more so, Mr Silva, even more so."

The solicitor's office reminded José of an old English stately home. The mahogany panelled walls hung with paintings of people long gone from this earth, shelves with volume after volume of law books, and a desk that would be worthy of a head of state. On a brown leather chair behind the desk was a distinguished gentleman, thin-faced, grey, almost white hair, and a pair of half-moon spectacles defying the laws of gravity, perched on the end of his nose.

Ask someone to draw a solicitor and this would be the man they drew thought José.

"Mr Silva, I need you to read this letter I have received from a firm of solicitors in the Caribbean. It will explain my need to establish your identity."

José took the letter and started to read. He stopped and looked at the solicitor.

"Am I reading this correctly?"

"You are indeed, Mr Silva, and may I be the first to congratulate you on your good fortune. It is not every day we have someone in our offices who has been bequeathed three million dollars. We are of course at your service for anything you may need."

"Yes...but I still don't understand," said José frowning "I don't know anybody in the Caribbean."

"It would appear somebody knew you."

José read the letter again and then something caught his eye.

After some time signing papers, discussing his future plans and financial matters, José finally left the offices of Gonzales and Barros stepped into the limousine for his return journey to Albufeira. He would have just enough time to prepare the evening food.

As they pulled out into the busy Portimão traffic José started to laugh. A rib-hurting, out-loud laugh, causing the driver to enquire if something was wrong.

"No, not at all. Everything is fine," he said with tears rolling down his cheeks.

What had caught his eye in the letter was the signature at the bottom. Almaz Kupets. Only a handful of people knew he could speak Russian. Almaz Kupets — Diamond Merchant.

They had pulled it off after all. Major José Duarte de Oliviera Silva was now a wealthy man.

CHAPTER SEVENTY-FOUR
29th July 1991, Canary Wharf, London.

Lenny sat at the desk that for so long had been occupied by Donald Munro. Mr Munro however, would not be needing his desk for a while. He was detained at Her Majesty's pleasure in Wandsworth Prison. Unfortunately for Donald some of his best enemies were serving time there too. None of the other men testified against him, they knew the power he could wield even from behind bars. The reporter on the other hand had been only too happy to take the witness stand. Although the evidence from him wasn't watertight, the jury had believed him and brought back a unanimous verdict.

Munro had always treated Lenny as the dumb muscle. Ultimately it led to his downfall. Being dumb also led to the demise of Eddie, in Harry Hart's offices. In this case Eddie had been the dumb one. Lenny knew acetylene bottles should not be stored on their sides. It would appear Eddie had not. The resultant fire had destroyed both Eddie and the offices. Of course Lenny had not left it to chance, and had sabotaged the rig to make sure it would blow. Lenny had a lot of knowledge of things the others were not aware of. With Eddie out of the way, Lenny had arranged a visit from Her Majesty's Constabulary to the offices of Donald Munro. Someone they had longed to arrest for many a year. They had been interested to hear Munro had counterfeit notes on his premises.

The bonus was seeing them arrest Willie for attempted murder. He never liked that man. Always looking down his nose at the 'Thicko'.

Lenny sat back and thought about the past five years of playing the dumb kid. He hadn't done too badly out of it. After Munro's arrest he had been quick to empty the offices of all the contents, and move them to his newly leased office in the recently opened Canary Wharf. Munro had always assumed Lenny was too stupid to notice anything and had been careless with passwords, bank account details and safe combinations. Lenny had taken full advantage, whilst maintaining his air of stupidity. He had managed to pull the wool over the eyes of everyone for five years, and his reward was to take a small fortune away from Munro. Pity he couldn't tell anyone. He chuckled. Speaking of pity, he pitied the poor constable who had been guarding the offices after Munro's arrest. When Lenny and his crew had turned up in a large Met Police truck, to 'remove the evidence for safekeeping', he had just allowed them to walk straight in, and out again with most of Munro's valuable possessions. Just goes to show if you have the brass neck you can get away with anything. Now he had a legitimate diamond business in the name of Leonard Stone, appropriate he thought. He had reverted to his mother's maiden name and his new found wealth had paid for the appropriate documents to go with it. Lenny Morvern had ceased to exist.

Lenny intended to stay on the 'strait and narrow' from now on. Greed had been the downfall of many, and Lenny did not intend to add to their ranks. Finally, he would be putting his education, and knowledge of gemstones to good use. Munro should not have put his father out of business. Had he not done so, his father would not have killed himself, and Lenny would have been a part of his business, father and son. Revenge, they say, is a dish best served cold. Lenny had waited until it had frozen over before serving it, but when he finally did, he served it with panache.

One mystery still remained for him. He had no idea how the money had been switched. He was almost certain it was something to do with Harry Hart, who had vanished from the face of the earth, but just how it had been achieved, he could not fathom at all. Still, good luck to him. He had unwittingly helped Lenny in setting up Munro for the fall.

Lenny poured himself a drink from his well-stocked bar and looked out across the dock towards London's newest airport. He raised his glass in salute. "Thank you Harry, wherever you are."

THE END

Glen R. Stansfield is a qualified aircraft engineer, a profession he has pursued for over forty years.

A lifelong interest in crime, in particular forensic psychology, led him to write his debut novel, *Fishing for Stones*.

Glen is working on his second novel, *Harry*, a tense thriller set in Kuwait and London.

When not writing, he can usually be found on two wheels, often using his motorcycle to raise money for charity.

His work has taken him to Bahrain, where he lives with his wife, Jess.

He looks forward to your comments, good or bad, and you can visit him at:

www.glen-r-stansfield.com

The Man in a Hat Publishing

FISHING FOR STONES